GRIMM HOUSE

Also by
KAREN McQUESTION

FOR YOUNGER READERS
Celia and the Fairies
Secrets of the Magic Ring

FOR OLDER READERS
Favorite
Life on Hold
From a Distant Star

The Edgewood Series
Edgewood
Wanderlust
Absolution

FOR ADULTS
A Scattered Life
Easily Amused
The Long Way Home
Hello Love

GRIMM HOUSE

Karen McQuestion

NIGHTSKY PRESS

Best wishes, Karen McQuestion

NIGHTSKY PRESS

Publisher's Note: This is a work of fiction. Names, characters, places, and incidents are a product of the author's imagination. Locales and public names are sometimes used for atmospheric purposes. Any resemblance to actual people, living or dead, or to businesses, companies, events, institutions, or locales is completely coincidental.

Cover art and design by Caitlin O'Dwyer

Interior illustrations by Caitlin O'Dwyer

www.caitlinodwyerillustration.com

ISBN 978-0986416477

Printed in the United States of America

For every kid who loves to read. You're the best.

CHAPTER 1

Hadley's parents had been gone three days when there was a knock on the door.

This was odd because her building had a doorman who also worked the front desk. Besides, there were cameras in the lobby. It would be hard to get past all that security without anyone noticing. Hadley and her parents lived in an apartment on the highest floor of Graham Place, the third floor, and never once in all their years living there had they ever gotten a visitor without first getting a call from the doorman.

The knock came again, this time louder. The babysitter, a high school girl named Zoe, didn't even look up from her phone. "Get that, would ya?" She tucked a piece of hair behind one ear and snapped her gum.

Hadley slid off the couch and went to the peephole. Because she was small for her age, she had to stand on her tippy toes to look straight through. On the other side of the door stood an old woman with storm-colored eyes, squinting as if she could see her too. Hadley took a step back. "Yes?" she asked. "Can I help you?"

The woman's voice was clear and forceful. "Is this the Brighton residence?"

Hadley looked to Zoe for guidance, but the babysitter was still absorbed in her phone, no doubt texting her boyfriend words of undying love. Hadley's parents had gone on a ten-day cruise and Zoe had promised to take good care of their daughter while they were gone. She'd stuck to her word, although not without grumbling. Sometimes Hadley overheard her talking on the phone. Zoe said she missed her boyfriend, hated the apartment, and thought Hadley was an immature little brat. Hearing those words made Hadley's eyes well up with tears. She missed her parents and had tried to stay out of Zoe's way. And she was *not* an immature brat. Not even close.

Hadley wasn't a brat. She was something else entirely. She was a dancer. When she was a baby, her feet had moved to the sound of music. As a toddler, she bypassed walking, going from crawling to dancing. When others her age were stumbling and bumbling, she moved gracefully across the floor. When she'd gotten old enough, she had taken dance lessons and practiced for hours every day. Her best friends, Sophia and Lily, were dancers too, and they were rivals in competitions, but never minded when one of the others won.

Dancing was so much a part of her life that there was a room in her apartment, empty except for a mirrored wall fronted by a ballet bar. Hadley's very own dance studio. The studio was what Zoe resented the most. "The kid has a room just for practicing her dancing," she whispered into the phone. "Can you believe it? Must be nice to be an only child." She laughed bitterly. "Nothing's too good for Hadley," she said in a mocking voice.

Hadley yelled from the next room, "I heard that." But Zoe didn't care.

When Hadley's mother and father found out they'd won two free tickets for a cruise, they debated going because they didn't want to leave their daughter behind. She overheard them discussing all the pros and cons. Finally they sat her down on the couch and explained the situation.

"It's only for a week," her father had said, "but if you don't want us to go, we will turn it down." He had his arm around Hadley's mom. She was a trim, elegant woman with a gentle nature, and now she smiled encouragingly at her daughter. Both of Hadley's parents delighted in her dancing talent and didn't mind writing the checks that funded her lessons and costumes.

Before every performance, her family had a routine. Her father insisted that the three of them embrace in what he called a Brighton family group hug. A cheesy tradition, but one she came to count on. After that, her mother would tell her how proud they were of her and say, "No one expects you to be perfect. Just do your best and make it matter." On stage, Hadley danced without worry, knowing her parents were devotedly watching from the audience.

They did so much for her that she didn't want to keep them from having fun on the cruise. Still, she had some concerns.

"But who would stay with me?" Hadley asked. She was old enough to be home alone for a few hours, but a whole week was something else entirely. "And who would take me to my dance classes?"

"We've thought of that," her mother said. "Remember Zoe who lives on the second floor? Her mother was just telling me she didn't have any luck getting a job this summer. She assured me that Zoe would love to stay here with you. Won't that be fun?"

Hadley could tell they really wanted to go, and so she said yes, it would be fun. Or at least fine. As it turned out though, Zoe was a pain. Right after Hadley's parents left, she overheard Zoe telling a friend on the phone that her family was moving out of their apartment soon. She was angry about having to move to another city, especially during her senior year of high school. All of her fury was aimed at her parents.

"I told them I'm just not going," she said crisply over the phone. "That's all there is to it."

Hadley's ears perked up at the next part. Zoe snapped her gum and said, "Supposedly the reason we're moving is because the building is being sold to some old guy. But he's not even raising the rent.

Nothing's going to change, so I don't know why that even matters."

But when Hadley asked about the building being sold and Zoe's upcoming move (and she'd only been trying to be nice), Zoe said, "Mind your own business."

In a way, Hadley understood. She herself wouldn't want to live anywhere else. She'd visited friends' homes and liked her apartment the best of all of them. The doormen were helpful and the other residents were friendly. Out of all of the tenants, she did have a few favorites. She liked being able to pet Mrs. Knapp's dog, Chester, when she met up with them in the lobby. Mr. Mumbles never complained about her dancing even though he lived right below them. And the two old ladies on the first floor, Miss Kenny and Miss Goodman, always came to her dance recitals and brought her flowers. Really, most everyone who lived in her apartment building was nice.

And besides that, Graham Place was simply beautiful. The building was old, but not run-down. Friends of her parents always commented on the high ceilings, beautiful cut-glass light fixtures, crown moldings, and gleaming floors. They marveled at the high-end finishes and unique architectural details. Hadley's bedroom ceiling had plaster crown molding running along the top of each wall. Unlike most decorative molding, Hadley's featured sculpted images of birds and flowers. Once, when her room was being painted, Hadley's father let her climb a ladder so she could run her fingers over the raised wings of a hummingbird. "It's incredible," she said with a sigh.

"One of a kind," her father told her. "None like it anywhere else. It was done just for this room. The artist came from Italy to do it when the place was first being built. We're lucky to live in a building with old-world charm."

Hadley didn't care about old-world charm. To her, Graham Place was just home.

Zoe was crabby by the second day and crabbier still on the third. She complained bitterly about Hadley's dancing, saying she couldn't stand the music and the thumping of her feet (there was no thumping as far as Hadley could tell). Because of this, she sent Hadley to practice down in the basement of the apartment building.

Hadley took the elevator down, carrying her iPod and speakers in a small zippered case. When she got to the first floor, she crossed the lobby and took the stairs down to the basement. Truthfully, the basement made her nervous. It was dim and dank, and filled with the sound of the clanking water boiler. Narrow windows on one side let in a bit of light. Otherwise, she had to depend on a few bare bulbs. She passed the furnace and the old incinerator. The incinerator had a wide mouth and reminded Hadley of the witch's oven in the Hansel and Gretel story. This particular incinerator was once used to burn all of the building's garbage, but ever since the city started garbage pickup, it had stood idle.

Every unit in the building had a storage room, the spaces divided by chicken wire, so she could see each family's possessions. Stacks of old furniture. A grandfather clock. Boxes and boxes and boxes stacked from the floor to the ceiling. A stuffed crow on a pedestal, which stared through the mesh as she went by. Hadley walked down the narrow corridor all the way to her own family's very empty storage space (her mother didn't want to store things in the damp, bug-infested basement), pulled on her shoes, then started her music and danced. It wasn't the same as practicing upstairs, but at least she wouldn't have to listen to Zoe's griping.

The next day, Hadley danced in the basement again, working hard to perfect her routine for the upcoming competition. When she was finally satisfied, she took a break, sipping from her water bottle and wiping the sheen of perspiration from her forehead. It was then she heard a knock at the window on the opposite side of the basement. The suddenness of it startled her, but when she saw it was a boy about her age, her fear melted.

"Hello," he yelled into the glass, waving from the other side. He was crouching inside the window well, something Hadley had always wanted to do but never did. She was a rule follower.

Hadley moved closer to the window. "What do you want?" she called out. She saw his face clearly now. Dark eyes framed by long lashes. A big smile made more noticeable by the braces on his teeth.

Now he pushed his shaggy hair out of his eyes. "Your dancing is awesome," he shouted, giving her a thumbs-up of approval. "Awesome!" Now she saw he wore a gray, well-worn T-shirt.

"Thank you." Hadley felt a strange mix of emotions. Annoyed that he had spied on her, but pleased to get a compliment.

"Can I come down and watch?"

"No," Hadley said. "I'm done now."

His disappointment was evident, but she didn't care. Even if he was a kid, he was a stranger and his request was weird. "Okay," he said, still yelling so she could hear. "I didn't want to bother you, but your dancing was so incredible I had to say something."

"Thank you," she said, going back to the storage area to gather up her things. When she came out, he was gone. She took the elevator up to the apartment, where she showered and changed clothes.

So this was twice in one day that she'd experienced a mystery knock. First the boy at the basement window and now this strange woman rapping on the apartment door, wanting to know if this was the Brighton residence. Hadley answered, "Yes, this is the Brighton residence. Who are you?"

The woman continued without answering her question. "I need to talk to whoever is in charge of the household, please." The please sounded like an afterthought. Even from the other side of the door, this woman had a commanding presence.

"Can you show some identification?" Hadley asked, using a line from a police show she'd once seen.

"Oh, for crying out loud," Zoe said, putting the phone down. She got up and strode to the door, disengaging the safety chain and yanking the door open. "Hello?" Zoe was several inches taller than Hadley, but appeared childlike next to this very tall woman.

"Yes, thank you. I will come in," the woman said, and Zoe stepped aside as if there were nothing unusual about this. Hadley felt the back of her neck prickle in alarm as the woman walked past, boots clicking on the marble floor, her black velvet cape fluttering as she went. She was statuesque and reedy with shoulder-length, curly gray hair and red-painted fingernails.

Hadley whispered, "We're not supposed to let strangers in," but Zoe only waved off her concerns.

"I'm Maxine Grimm," the woman said, reaching out to shake Zoe's hand. "I'm this little girl's great-aunt. I'm afraid I have some sad news."

"Some sad news?" Zoe repeated, while Hadley was thinking—*great-aunt? I didn't know I had a great-aunt.*

She looked at the woman for signs of a family resemblance. Maxine Grimm was tall and thin like both of her parents, but that's where the similarity ended. Hadley's parents were lively and quick to laugh. Judging from the frown lines on this woman's face, laughing wasn't something she was familiar with. Her gray hair too was odd. Curled like a doll from the 1800s, it fell in springs across her shoulders. No one had hair like that anymore.

"Oh, such sad, sad news," Maxine said, wringing her skeletal hands. "I almost can't bear to tell you." She reached over, gave Hadley's shoulder a squeeze and sighed heavily. "It's tragic, really."

Hadley wriggled out of her grasp. "What is it?"

But Maxine was only talking to Zoe. "I got the phone call this morning, and I rushed right over. There's no easy way to say this, so I'll just put it out there. It seems the girl's parents are lost at sea. Their cruise ship capsized. Right now, both of them are unaccounted for." She pulled a lacy white handkerchief out of her pocket and dabbed at her eyes.

"You gotta be kidding," Zoe said, her eyes wide.

"I wish I were." Maxine sniffed.

Hadley felt her throat tighten but managed to croak out a few words. "My mom and dad... are dead?"

"Maybe. Maybe not," Maxine said, folding the handkerchief into a neat square and tucking it back into her pocket. "But since they're unaccounted for, everyone thought it would be best if you stayed with relatives until we know more. Hadley, you're coming home with me."

Hadley shook her head. "But I just talked to them last night." They'd called saying they loved and missed her. And now they were gone? She blinked back tears. This couldn't be true. Any minute, she'd find out that it was all a mistake and that this woman had come to the wrong apartment.

"Sometimes that happens," Maxine said. "You talk to people one day, and the next day you find out their ship has capsized. That's life."

"Gosh, that's terrible," Zoe said. "I didn't really know Mr. and Mrs. Brighton, but they seemed really nice." She took the news rather well. Too well, Hadley thought, but of course, it wasn't *her* parents who were missing.

"I just can't believe it," Hadley said. "I *don't* believe it."

"Denial," Maxine said, patting Hadley on the back. "It's one of the signs of grieving."

"How are you related to me again?" she asked.

"I'm your great-aunt on your mother's side." The businesslike way she said it suggested the subject was now closed.

"What happens now?" Zoe asked.

"I'll take it from here," Maxine said, pulling a thick wad of money from the pocket of her cape. "I do believe this will cover what you're owed for babysitting." She pressed a stack of bills into Zoe's hand. "If you can help pack a bag for the girl, we'll be on our way."

CHAPTER 2

Later, Hadley couldn't remember how she'd gotten to Grimm House. After the knock on the door, her memory became fuzzy. She did know that the babysitter, Zoe, happy to be rid of her, had quickly filled a suitcase with Hadley's clothes along with her dance shoes. Zoe had given Aunt Maxine and Hadley a quick wave goodbye before darting out the door. Hadley remembered not wanting to go with the woman. She asked, "How do I know you're my aunt? My parents never mentioned you."

Aunt Maxine chuckled. "Children are such horrible, messy things. Who would take one if they didn't have to?"

At the time, it seemed like a satisfactory answer, but later, Hadley wasn't sure at all. It was all so confusing. She asked if she could call her parents, but Aunt Maxine said she'd just tried and there was no answer. When she saw that Hadley was about to cry, Maxine pulled her into an awkward hug and patted her back. "There, there, now. Everything is going to be fine. Just fine." After the hug, Hadley seemed to lose control of her arms and legs. She felt pulled along as if there were a rope tied around her waist.

Aunt Maxine carried her suitcase down the hall to the elevator with Hadley following mutely behind. When they reached the dark green car (was it in front of the building? Somehow Hadley couldn't recall), the older woman asked, "Would you like to ride in the backseat or get strapped to the top?"

Hadley said, "In the backseat, I guess."

"Have it your way," Aunt Maxine said, humming a little tune and ushering her through the car door.

Was it a long car ride? Hadley wasn't sure. She thought she'd fallen asleep at some point. It must have been quite a while, because when they arrived it was dark. She woke up with a cramped neck just as they pulled up to Aunt Maxine's house. "Finally," Aunt Maxine muttered as they came to a stop right by the front door.

Another woman came out as they exited the car. She peered at Hadley with dark, deep-set eyes. She looked like a somewhat thinner version of Aunt Maxine. "Is this the one? The little dancer?" The woman clasped her hands together with delight.

"I'm Hadley," she said, clutching the handle of her suitcase.

"Of course you are," the woman said. "You can call me Aunt Charmaine. I'm Maxine's younger sister."

Aunt Charmaine helped the groggy Hadley out of the car and steered her into the house while Aunt Maxine followed with her suitcase. "What is this place?" Hadley asked, looking around the dark paneled entryway.

"This is our home," Aunt Charmaine said. "Welcome to Grimm House."

The entrance at Grimm House had once been majestic, but now dust covered the woodwork and the walls were scuffed and dented. An elegant staircase with marble steps curved up to the second floor. A grandfather clock stood next to a coat tree, empty except for an umbrella hanging from one of the hooks. "Your clock has no hands," Hadley observed.

Aunt Charmaine said, "Clocks that tell time are only important for people in a hurry. Here at Grimm House we have plenty of time."

Aunt Maxine shut the door behind them and pulled a key out of her pocket. The locking mechanism made a thunk as she secured the front door from the inside. She shook off her cape, and Hadley saw she wore a dress identical to her sister's. Light blue in color and nearly floor length, it had rows of white lace running from the neckline to the waist. The collar was rounded, and the sleeves were puffy, like on a baby's dressing gown.

The windows on either side of the front door were reinforced with decorative metal bars. The door itself was massive and rounded on top. Hadley's eyes widened as she looked at everything in the front hall. It reminded her of a medieval castle.

"You'd think the child had never been inside a nice house before," Aunt Maxine said to her sister, one hand on her hip.

"Now, now, sister. No need to insult our guest," Aunt Charmaine said. She leaned over and looked Hadley in the eye. "Let's go inside and get you settled."

The aunts gave her a tour, leading her through hallways lined with paintings of serious-looking people, most of them old men who looked down on Hadley disapprovingly. When she walked past, she felt their eyes following her. Wallpaper lined every surface. Stripes and polka dots and roses as big as a head of lettuce. Looking at all the patterns made her dizzy. Each of the windows was framed by heavy tapestry drapes held back by gold cords, the kind seen in funeral homes and old movies.

The first floor consisted of the entryway, parlor, kitchen, and formal dining room. She understood the layout of the first floor, but as they rose up the staircase to the next floor, things got weirder. The second story, as far as she could tell, was a maze of rooms, most of them cluttered with dusty possessions. She couldn't keep track of all of them except to pick one particular detail which then defined the room for her. One by one, she named them. The room with the stuffed crow under a domed glass cover. The one with the bookcases and the carved totem pole. The room with the peeling paint. The one with all the mirrors. The room filled with mannequins wearing military uniforms.

"You have some unusual things," Hadley said, trying to be polite.

"Yes," Aunt Charmaine said proudly. "So many wonderful things."

The third floor consisted of a bathroom and bedrooms. She only had to be concerned with one bedroom, Aunt Maxine said, opening a doorway. "This will be your room while you're here." Inside was the plainest bedroom Hadley had ever seen. Walls, a bed, and a dresser. The bed was covered with a thin green blanket frayed on the edges. The pillow was flat and gray, like the pillowcase hadn't been washed in a very long time. The wooden dresser leaned to one side and the blue painted walls were cracked and chipped. Aunt Maxine continued, wagging her finger at Hadley. "You're lucky to get your own room, believe me. If we weren't so nice, you'd be sleeping on the floor in the kitchen."

"Where do the two of you sleep?" Hadley asked.

"We each have a room down the hall, not that it's any of your business."

"Oh, sister," Aunt Charmaine said. "Let's be nice. The little monkey didn't mean any harm. Did you, dear?"

"No," Hadley said, shaking her head.

"Still." Aunt Maxine frowned. "You need to know that we need our sleep and don't want to be disturbed. None of this crying for Mommy or any of that nonsense. Keep it to yourself."

They proceeded to the end of the hallway, where Aunt Charmaine pointed out one last thing. She tapped on a closed door and said, "This leads up to the attic. You must never, ever go into the attic for any reason. You have no business being up there, and if we discover you nosing around in the attic, you will be punished."

"Severely punished," Aunt Maxine added with a sniff. "It will be the end of you, and I mean that exactly as it sounds."

"You probably wouldn't want to go up there anyway," Aunt Charmaine added. "It's dirty and hot."

"Severely punished," Aunt Maxine repeated. "It will be the end of you."

"I won't go up there," Hadley promised.

"Now that we've gone to the top, let's head down to the bottom," Aunt Charmaine said, leading the way down one staircase and then another and then another until they reached the basement. When they got to the bottom of the stairs, Hadley drew back in horror. Cobwebs hung in sweeping arches and dust motes swam lazily in the dim light. Just walking through the space made her feel icky. "The place hasn't been cleaned in quite some time," Aunt Charmaine said, as if that needed to be pointed out. "So I was thinking that could be your project this summer."

"Me?" Hadley asked.

"Of course she means you," Aunt Maxine said. "My sister and I don't do that kind of dirty work. It's disgusting. Mucking about in the grime and filth is work for children." She sniffed again. "Besides, there are bugs down here, and I'm allergic to bugs."

"You're allergic to everything." Aunt Charmaine swept aside a cobweb and stepped up to a large metal bin resembling a Dumpster. "Here's something you don't see every day, Hadley. This is our dustbin." She knocked on the top, and a slight echo bounced off the basement walls. "It's one of our proudest possessions."

Hadley asked, "What's in there?"

"The result of a lot of hard work," Aunt Charmaine said cheerfully. "Dust, soot, and other ashy things."

"What do you do with it?" Hadley asked.

"What do you mean, child?"

"How do you throw it out if it's down here in the basement?"

Aunt Charmaine gasped. "What a ridiculous question. We don't waste things in this house. Everything that goes in the dustbin stays in the dustbin. It's our collection, so it's important to us. Sometimes I like to just come down and look at it. For right now, you just need to know that it has a special place here in the basement."

Aunt Maxine added, "You'll have no reason to use the dustbin. Just leave it be."

The tour over, they trooped up the stairs to the first floor, and just like that, Hadley's life changed. She was once a cherished daughter and girl with many friends. Now she was a lonely child in an odd place. Grimm House had a climate of its own. Even though it was summer, the house was as chilly and damp as a cave. When Hadley's hand brushed against the wallpaper, it felt damp, and the carpet runner squished when she stepped on it. The air hung heavy with cold humidity.

The aunts believed in discipline and schedules, so they told her she was expected down to breakfast by six o'clock. Because there were no clocks in the house (aside from the handless grandfather clock in the front hall), Hadley got up when she heard the aunts start their day. She washed her face in the bathroom using the rough washcloth and sour-smelling soap, then brushed her teeth with her finger since Zoe had forgotten to pack her toothbrush. Once she was presentable, she made her way down the two flights of stairs and greeted the aunts who were already in the kitchen.

When Aunt Maxine fixed breakfast the first morning, she showed Hadley how it was done, turning on the gas burner and then lighting it with a match. She melted butter in a heavy iron skillet. After that, she expertly cracked eggs into the pan and then turned to the ice box, pulling out a large wedge of bacon. She quickly cut off a few slices and tossed them next to the eggs in the skillet.

"We don't have an ice box at home," Hadley commented. "We have a refrigerator."

"No one cares, little girl," she said. "Watch carefully. You'll need to know how to do this."

After that, it was Hadley's job. "It's important for a girl to know how to prepare a meal," Aunt

Charmaine said approvingly, piling her plate with bacon. "Good job, you silly little goose."

Aunt Maxine said, "Hadley, these eggs are a little runny. Tomorrow you'll have to do better."

The rest of the day's routine involved quiet time (when the aunts napped), cleaning (Hadley dusted and scrubbed while the aunts supervised), and outdoor time, where she was allowed to go outside by herself for one full hour. The backyard was filled with trees and surrounded with a wooden fence too high for even the tallest person to see over; it was definitely too high to climb.

The first time she went outside, Hadley walked the perimeter of the yard, looking for a gate, but the yard was completely enclosed. After that, she used her outdoor time to get some fresh air, but alas, the air outside was nearly as musty and damp as in the house. She had never known such gloomy summer days. The sky above Grimm House was crinkled and gray, a depressing sight. She longed to see the sun.

As far as she could tell, the aunts never left the house. Groceries and other supplies appeared on the front porch. For entertainment, they talked to each other, squabbling like children and laughing like hyenas. "Remember the time…," Aunt Maxine would start out and then bring up some embarrassing thing her sister had done years before.

"You would say that!" was Aunt Charmaine's favorite reply. "You mean old thing."

In their youth, they'd both liked the same boys, and they blamed each other for the fact that they'd ended up alone. "George said I was the prettiest thing he ever laid eyes on," Aunt Charmaine said. "I could have had him for a boyfriend if you hadn't ruined things."

Aunt Maxine scoffed. "You live in a dream world, Charmaine. He never said any such thing."

"Oh, yes, he did!"

"Oh, no, he didn't!"

"The prettiest thing he ever saw! It's true. That's what he said. I heard it with my own ears."

"Those ears? The ones that flap so much it looks like you borrowed them from an elephant?"

"Oh Maxine, you're just too awful to live. If you weren't my dear sister, I wouldn't talk to you ever again!" The words were harsh, but she didn't sound angry. Insulting each other was what they did for fun.

Hadley listened to them laugh and squawk at each other, and loneliness washed over her. How she wished she could talk to her friends, Sophia and Lily. At this point, she'd even want to have Zoe as a babysitter again. But the aunts didn't have a phone, and she was forbidden to leave. All the doors leading outdoors were kept locked as were the windows. Hadley wondered what the aunts were trying to keep out.

Her favorite part of the day came after the evening meal, when she was allowed to dance. Zoe, who had neglected to send a toothbrush, had somehow remembered to pack all of Hadley's dance recital outfits. Having them with her at the aunts' house brought her comfort. Every evening she held them up, one at a time, trying to decide which one to wear.

Each costume held memories of a performance, and because of this, each one carried an emotion with it. One she associated with a jazzy number, another with a dramatic slow dance. Yet another costume reminded her of a dance duet she'd done with Lily. The culmination of hours of work had built into a stellar performance, every move perfectly in sync. The bond of friendship was made even stronger by the shared love of dancing.

As a little girl, she'd immediately taken to dance lessons because she was naturally good at it, but as time went on, it was the other dancers who drove her to practice and improve. Her mother said she'd found her tribe, and it was true. Hadley had found her tribe, and it was the best tribe she could ever imagine having.

The outfits spread out on the bed reminded her of this and made her smile. She took her time choosing, admiring the sequins and the sheen of the stretchy spandex. Once she'd dressed, her mood lifted and she was ready to go downstairs and dance. Hearing the swish of the tulle skirt as she bounded down the stairs brought back the anticipation she felt every time she crossed a stage.

The aunt's parlor was the perfect room for a performance, with a large open space in the middle of the room right underneath a gorgeous crystal chandelier. A large library table holding a lamp was positioned in front of a window, out of the way of the dancing area. For music, Aunt Charmaine wound up an old-fashioned record player she called a Victrola. Once she put the needle on the record and the music began, she and Aunt Maxine settled into overstuffed armchairs and watched as Hadley spun and twirled to the music. Hour after hour of joyful dancing. It was the only time she felt like herself. The aunts urged her on until she danced herself into exhaustion. She had an occasional misstep, but nothing could deter her spirit.

"Wonderful, Hadley, wonderful!" Aunt Maxine called out.

"Bravo, bravo." Aunt Charmaine blew kisses her way.

Their clapping and cheering kept her going even when her feet hurt and her muscles ached. Getting up the stairs to bed was always a problem, but falling asleep afterward came easy.

In the morning, she'd wake up remembering why she was there. She missed her parents and her old life. At breakfast, she'd ask about her mother and father. "Any news about the ship? Have you heard anything about my parents?"

At first the aunts were kind, telling her tidbits of information about the rescue efforts.

"The Coast Guard is on the case," Aunt Maxine told her. "The search-and-rescue team is out every single day."

"Don't worry, Hadley," Aunt Charmaine had said at one point. "There are so many small islands in that region. Your parents are probably on one of them just waiting to be discovered!"

Hadley tried to imagine her fun-loving parents stranded on a deserted island. They'd be tired and dirty but making the best of things. She imagined her mother, ever the clever one, figuring out how to crack open coconuts while her father fished for their dinner.

Soon enough, they'd be rescued. And when that happened, they'd come to Grimm House to take her home. Being home would be such a relief. With her parents on either side of her at the kitchen table, she could eat cereal for breakfast and not have to worry about lifting the heavy cast-iron skillet onto the big stove and getting the eggs just right.

After a while, the aunts became impatient with her questions. "Enough already, Hadley," Aunt Maxine snapped, her teeth gleaming. "If there's any news, we'll tell you."

"You never let up," Aunt Charmaine said. "Always asking. Every single day you have to keep bringing it up."

"My parents, my parents, my parents," Aunt Maxine whined. "It's like a bad song no one wants to hear."

Hadley swallowed the lump in her throat. "I'm sorry."

Seeing her worried look, Aunt Charmaine softened and said, "Don't worry, little girl. If anyone can figure out what to do, it would be your father. Even as a child, he was always such a clever boy."

The words hung in the air while Hadley thought. "But," she said, "I thought you said you were my mother's aunt." Aunt Charmaine's face hardened into a mask of irritation. Hadley went on. "Isn't that what you said?" She turned to Aunt Maxine. "Didn't you say you were related to me on my mother's side?"

Aunt Maxine rolled her eyes. "You handle this one, Charmaine," she said in disgust. "You stepped in it. You fix it."

Aunt Charmaine sighed. "Hadley, you are such a ditzy girl. Of course we're related on your mother's side. But that doesn't mean I didn't know your father when he was a child. I knew him from the neighborhood. He was a pistol, that one."

"But my father grew up in another state," Hadley said. She'd always loved the story of how her parents had met on the first day of college. Her father had spotted her mother at orientation and knew right away she was the one for him. "I don't understand how you would have known him when he was a little boy."

"He came to visit the area, of course," Aunt Charmaine said. "On vacation."

"What's his name then, if you knew him?"

Aunt Charmaine gave her a blank look and then said, "That's not the issue here, and you are being rude, young lady."

"I don't think you're telling the truth. I don't think you ever knew him at all," Hadley said. She blinked back the start of tears. "I want to go home. You need to let me go."

"You're not going anywhere, young lady," Charmaine said, pointing a bony finger her way.

Still, Hadley kept at it. "You need to call my other relatives to come and get me. I want to go home."

"Enough!" Aunt Maxine roared. "Don't you see how you're upsetting Charmaine?" And indeed, Charmaine did look put out, her mouth turned down in a rather sullen way. "Go outside, girl, and leave us in peace."

Hadley got up from the table to follow orders, but Aunt Maxine yanked at the back of her shirt as she went by. "Where do you think you're going? I didn't mean to go outside right now," she said. "You can go after you do the cleanup. These dishes aren't going to wash themselves, you know."

Aunt Charmaine added, "And don't forget to sweep. I can't abide crumbs on the floor."

"After that, you can sweep the basement floor," Aunt Maxine said.

"And while you're down there, you can use the broom to knock down all the cobwebs," Aunt Charmaine added and in an aside to her sister said, "That will teach the little ankle biter to mouth off to her elders."

The aunts walked out, leaving Hadley to carry the dishes to the sink. At the apartment, there was a dishwasher, but here everything was done by hand. She had learned to save the skillet for last because otherwise the grease in the dishwater made it difficult to get the dishes clean. Now she took her time, carefully rinsing and wiping each piece dry. In the other room, she overheard her aunts' discussion. Hadley paused to listen.

"The impudence!" Aunt Charmaine hissed. "We give the girl a home. We feed her and watch over her, and she dares to question me? We haven't had such a sassy one in a long while."

"She's been a problem right from the start," Aunt Maxine said in a rather loud whisper. "I usually don't have so much trouble with children. The girl actually said she didn't believe me when I told her the ship capsized. Came right out and said she doubted me. Can you believe it?"

"Well, it is a bit unbelievable."

"Really?" Aunt Maxine said with a sniff. "I actually thought it was one of my better stories."

There was a long pause, and then the voices became quieter. Hadley strained to listen but only caught a few words. Ingrate. Dancing. Prisms. None of it made sense. Then Aunt Charmaine said, "At least it will be over soon. With the way she dances, I'd think it would be no more than a week or two."

Aunt Maxine sniffed. "If she even lasts that long. I've never seen such passion in a child. I can't wait until it's ours."

CHAPTER 3

Once Hadley had finished the dishes, she took a broom to the floor, careful to sweep up every last bit. When she was finished gathering up the crumbs, she couldn't find a garbage can, so she swept them into the corner. Later she would ask how to dispose of it. From the other room, the sound of the aunts' shrill laughter pierced the air. "Not much longer," Aunt Charmaine said in a sing-songy voice. "And the passion will be ours."

Aunt Maxine joined in, chirping, "Not much longer and the passion will be ours."

"Not much longer and the passion will be ours!" Together they repeated it over and over again, their voices becoming music that wasn't music. The words rose and fell, causing a chill up Hadley's spine. It was a tribal war chant. The whine of bumblebees spiraling to their death. A strong wind coming to knock down everything in its path. The voices of the two aunts sounded like all those things and more.

"Not much longer and the passion will be ours!" The aunts sang the words and shrieked with laughter in between.

Hadley quietly left the room and headed down to the basement with the broom and dustpan in hand. Getting away from them gave her time to think. What did they mean by saying the passion would become theirs? She thought they were kind of old to become dancers. And what did Aunt Maxine mean when she said she thought that her parents' ship capsizing was one of her better stories? If that wasn't the truth, what was? Had something even worse happened to her parents, something they didn't want to tell her?

And another thing—why did they say Hadley would only last a week or two? She brightened suddenly, thinking of a good reason. Perhaps they were tiring of her and would drive her to another relative's house to get rid of her. She must have other relatives. Hadley was sure of that, but she found it so hard to remember.

She thought she'd once had grandparents and maybe an aunt and uncle too. A few cousins, maybe? She squinted, trying to remember. And if she did have other relatives, wouldn't it make more sense for her to be with them instead of some great-aunts she'd never met before? Every day she was less sure of the details of her life before she came to Grimm House. Her mind played such tricks; it was all so confusing. She wanted to write things down, thinking that might help to make things straight in her head, but Aunt Charmaine had said they didn't have any writing utensils or spare paper in the house. What a shame.

At the bottom of the basement stairs, she flipped on the light switch and wove her way around the dangling cobwebs, wincing as they brushed against her face. Even with the light on, it was hard to see. From the far end of the basement, she heard a faint noise. For a moment she stopped with the dustpan and broom still in hand. Didn't one of the aunts say there were bugs in the basement? She was not a fan of bugs.

She listened intently. There it was again—a noise like a sigh. Or maybe a whispering? "Who's there?" she called out, her voice trembling. Again she heard the sound of something rustling ahead. "I don't think this is funny. Come out right now." Her voice reverberated back to her, and she tilted her head to one side, listening. There was no one there, of course. In all the time she'd been in the aunts' house, she hadn't spotted another person. There was no one else in the basement. There couldn't be. It was just her imagination playing tricks on her.

Upstairs, the aunts' voices subsided, and she heard footsteps overhead. When she was finished with the basement, she'd remind them that they'd said she could go outside. Maybe this time she'd find a way to climb over the fence. Hadley had no idea if there were neighbors nearby, but if she walked long enough, she had to find someone. Outside help was the ticket to getting home. It was the someone elses of the world who might have a phone. And a phone was all she needed to reach her parents or the police.

Yes, now that Hadley had a little bit of a plan, she felt better. No more asking about her parents. Being near the aunts made her tired and confused. Things weren't adding up. She needed to take charge and try to get away from them.

But first to sweep the basement. Hadley walked from end to end, knocking down cobwebs with the broom. Most of them were straggly, gray things, long abandoned by their makers. But there was still one in use. One particular web hung in the corner, a large black-and-gold spider sitting regally in the center. Hadley wasn't fond of spiders, but she didn't see the point of destroying the web. It was beautiful in its own way. "You're safe for now," she told the spider. "You can thank me later."

Once she'd downed all the cobwebs, she got to work on the floor, sweeping methodically to make sure she didn't miss any spots. There was nothing complicated about it; in fact, it was downright boring, so she started to incorporate a few dance moves, using the broom as her partner. Without giving it any thought, she began to hum, delighted when she realized the song was from one of her past routines. She alternated between sweeping and dancing with the broom, smiling at the handle as she circled around it.

In class, Miss Lavinia had stressed the importance of smiling when dancing. "Let the audience know that you are enjoying yourself." And before competitions, she'd warn them, "Some judges will mark you down if you aren't smiling, so let's turn those frowns upside down!"

Smiling while dancing came easily for Hadley. Her father always said she looked like she was on top of the world. If only he could see her now, she thought. In a basement, grimy and covered with dust, a broom in her hand. At home she washed her hands the minute there was a speck of dirt on them, and here she was filthy from head to toe. Her father wouldn't recognize her. Hadley-ella. That's who she'd become.

She was leaning on the broom, lost in thought, when she heard that noise again. Very faint. A sigh or maybe a whisper? "Is someone there?" she called out, although she knew that wasn't possible. She'd swept the basement from corner to corner and hadn't encountered anyone. She was alone.

Hadley held her breath. There it was again! A sorrowful sigh. She followed the noise to the far side of the basement and lifted the metal cover of the dustbin. Inside the bin it was dark as ash, but she sensed something else too, and then she felt it as a wave of sadness rose out of the dustbin and hit her square in the face. Along with the feeling came the audible sound of sighing. Shocked, she dropped the lid of the dustbin and it clattered shut, stopping the sound. Her free hand rose to her mouth. The bin was full of dust and soot and was in front of a concrete wall. Was someone inside? How could that be? They wouldn't be able to breathe. She set the dustpan on the floor and lifted the lid once again. Again, she heard the sigh, and at the same time, she felt a pang of loss.

"Who are you?" Hadley asked. But there was no response. She stood there for the longest time until she wondered if she were imagining things. After all, basements were dark and dreary, and the sound of sighing was nearly no sound at all. "This doesn't make any sense. I think I am losing my mind," she said, half to herself. She shut the lid to the bin.

From the floor, she heard a voice, this one loud and clear. "Whaddya expect? You're talking to dirt. It's not going to make sense."

Hadley shrieked. "Who said that?" Down at her feet, she saw the floor move, but in another instant, she realized it wasn't the floor, but a million beetles, all of them with glowing green eyes. If she moved even an inch, she would step on them. She couldn't decide if she should run like the wind or stay absolutely still. For now she was frozen in place. "Who said that?" she repeated. "Who's talking?"

"It's me," said one of the bugs, scuttling up the dust bin until it got to the top. "The name's Gigi. I'm the one that's talking."

"Bugs can't talk," she said, pulling her hand back. If the thing jumped on her, she was going to scream her head off. A crawly feeling traveled up her spine. "It's a fact that bugs can't talk."

"Neither can a dustbin full of ashes, but I just watched you chatting it up there a minute ago."

Hadley said, "It's impossible for insects to talk. You don't have vocal chords."

The bug chittered out a laugh. "And yet I am. Talking, that is. Words are coming out of me and going out into the air, reaching your ears. Explain that, young one."

"It's a trick." She looked around the basement, looking for an explanation. Hidden speakers or someone talking from behind a pillar? "It has to be a trick."

"A pretty good trick," the bug agreed.

"Or else I'm imagining it."

"You do have an excellent imagination."

Up close, Hadley noticed the bug's hairy antennae and the stick legs protruding out of a fat, shiny body. Her green eyes glowed like lights. Hadley had never liked bugs, not even the friendly variety, and this one seriously weirded her out. Her stomach twisted, and she thought she was going to be sick.

The bug rose up on its back legs and gestured wildly. "Look, it's me, Gigi! I'm waving at you! How much more proof do you need?"

"I just want you to go away," she said. "Stop talking to me." I'm in a bad dream, she thought, closing her eyes. A horrible nightmare. If she pinched herself really, really hard, she'd wake up back in the apartment with Zoe the babysitter who didn't seem that mean after all. "This isn't happening. This isn't happening," she muttered to herself, gripping the skin on her wrist.

"Oh, it's happening all right," the bug said. On the floor below, the other bugs murmured in agreement. "Happening, happening, happening." Chitter, chitter, chatter. The bug added, "And I'm as real as you are."

"I don't like bugs," she said, her eyes still closed. "And you're freaking me out. Go away."

"We're not just any bugs," said the one on top of the dustbin. Did she say her name was Gigi? "We are the newest, best kind of roach, recently settled here from Florida. We could be the best friends you have in this house. We're smart and nearly indestructible. We can hide so cleverly that millions of us can live alongside humans virtually undetected. We are also excellent at adapting. As far as friends go, you could do far worse, believe me."

"I don't need any friends, thank you," Hadley said. Not any bug friends anyway. Just thinking about roaches made her skin crawl.

"That dirt you were talking to?"

"Yes?"

"There's nothing there. What you're getting from the dustbin would be the last vestiges of regret and loss."

"I don't get it."

The bug shrugged, her little shell going up and down. "It's part of human nature—longing for what might have been. Whole lives have been wasted, devoured by regret."

"I still don't understand. You're not making sense."

"I could tell you what happens in this house, but you won't believe me. I've tried before, and no one ever believes me."

Now Hadley was curious. "What do you mean, no one ever believes you? What are you talking about?"

"You're not the first kid in this house, ya know," Gigi said.

Down at Hadley's feet the rest of the bugs echoed her words. "Not the first! Oh no, not the first at all."

"We've seen them come. We've seen 'em go."

The insects on the floor: "Seen them come. Seen 'em go. Come and go, come and go."

There had been other children here before? Hadley's body went rigid. "There were other kids? What happened to them?"

Gigi said, "All of them had a talent, like you with your dancing. Some sang, some played musical instruments." She cocked her head to one side, thinking. "There was a boy who did magic tricks. He was pretty good, actually. Could have gone far with that. Maybe even pro. Las Vegas? I don't know. I'm just talking now. Anyhow, they did their talent every night for the witches, and then one night—poof! All that was left was ashes. And then the witches sweep up the ashes and put them in the bin." The bugs down below chittered until Gigi motioned to them to be quiet.

Hadley put a hand on her hip. "So the aunts are witches who turn kids into ashes? Like what, they burn the kids up?"

"No, no, no. The kids still live. The ashes are what's left after the witches suck the talent out of them. The ashes are a longing for what might have been. The ashes are the void you feel when you don't have your passion anymore."

Hadley felt a headache pushing its way against her forehead. Oh, why was she in a creepy basement where ashes sighed and insects confused her? "I'm going upstairs now," she said. "So you might all want to move before I step on you."

"Clear a path! Clear a path!" The bugs babbled and chattered, and magically the hordes of green-lit eyes scuttled to either side until there was a girl-sized path leading from the dustbin all the way to the stairs. She stooped to pick up the dustpan now mounded with dirt and then walked quickly through the opening.

Gigi called from behind her, "We could be your friends."

The other bugs chimed in all at once: "Friends, friends, friends!"

"It's a very good offer. Think about it," Gigi said.

"I don't need friends, thank you," she said. As if a bunch of roaches could take the place of Lily and Sophia.

Gigi yelled out, her voice thin but clear: "Can I at least give you some advice? Good advice. Free for the taking."

Hadley stopped in her tracks and turned her head to look. "What kind of advice?"

"The best kind of advice. The kind that will help."

Hadley thought for a second as she watched specks of dust swirl in front of her. Finally she answered. "Okay, I'm listening."

"Go up to the attic. That's where you'll find your answers."

"What's in the attic?"

"Just go. You'll see," Gigi said.

CHAPTER 4

Aunt Charmaine wasn't happy to see Hadley coming up from the basement. "What in the world were you doing downstairs?" she asked, frowning. "You have no business down there."

Hadley held out the dustpan. "You told me to sweep and knock down the cobwebs. I don't know where to dump the dirt, though."

"You numbskull." She grabbed the dustpan out of Hadley's hand and marched across the kitchen to a strip of metal mounted on the wall. Lifting the metal flap, she dumped the crumbs into the opening. "What did you think this was for?"

"I really didn't know," Hadley said, hanging her head. She hadn't even noticed the metal slot in the wall until that very moment. Things in this house just suddenly appeared. Like just now she saw with surprise that the kitchen floor was made up of hexagon-shaped tiles reminding her of a honey comb. Had it always been like that?

"Well, you can't help being a stupid-head, I guess," Aunt Charmaine said with a heavy sigh. Despite the name-calling, she was the nicer of the two sisters.

"I did my chores. Can I go outside now?" Hadley asked. Usually she was only allowed one hour outdoors every day, and that came after lunch, but she was hoping for an exception. "Aunt Maxine said I should go outside after my chores were done."

"She did say that, didn't she?" Aunt Charmaine tapped at her mouth with one finger. "Okay then." She pulled a key out of her pocket and unlocked the back door. "Get some fresh air in your lungs, Missy.

Suck up that oxygen. You'll need it when you dance tonight."

Hadley felt a surge of gratitude. "Thank you."

"And when you hear us calling, come in immediately."

"I will. I promise." Hadley nodded and ran out, glad to be free from the house at last. Inside were two crazy old ladies, a sad dustbin sighing with regret, and a swarm of roaches with glowing eyes who wanted to be her friends. Outside, somewhere in the world, there was her home and news of her parents. It was all still out there: Lily, Sophia, her family, her apartment, her neighbors. All of it waiting for her. If only she could figure out a way to get there.

The skies overhead were gray and overcast, no sun or clouds in sight, just as it had been ever since she arrived. The air was damp and musty. An odd fog swirled all around. She couldn't remember a summer with less sunshine. Filling her lungs with air, she tried to keep her mind sharp. Gigi had said the attic held answers for her, but she wasn't looking for answers. She was looking for a way home. Besides, how trustworthy was a roach? She could have told her the wrong thing on purpose. Maybe the roaches were in league with the aunts and were testing her to see if she'd disobey their rule about never going in the attic. Or maybe the roach really was trying to help her. There was no way to know for sure. So much to think about.

Her best bet, she thought, was to escape. She needed to flee from this place, get as far away as possible and beg strangers for help. Hadley tried to come up with a plan. She knew that every door that led outside was kept locked. The windows too were locked and were also fortified with metal crosspieces. It was only outdoors that she had any freedom at all.

With this in mind, Hadley followed the wooden fence around the perimeter of the yard. She pressed on each board, looking for a weakness, and kicked at the bottom, hoping to find a rotted spot. Climbing was out of the question. The fence was too high, and none of the trees were close to the edge of the lot. The yard was its own sort of prison.

Still Hadley kept going, pressing on boards and kicking at the bottoms, counting as she went. She tried scooping the dirt at the base of the fence, thinking she might be able to tunnel her way underneath. But without some kind of shovel or spade, it was nearly impossible. In fifteen minutes, she had only created a gap large enough for a small mouse to pass through. Doing the math, Hadley figured it would take hours and hours to make a girl-sized hole. She sighed. She just didn't have that kind of time.

She stood up and brushed the dirt from her hands, then continued on, glad that the trees and foliage shielded her from the house. If the aunts had a clue as to what she was doing, there would be big trouble. On and on she went. When she reached the 287th board, she noticed a huge knot in the wood, right at eye level. The lines in the board surrounding the knot actually made it look like an eye was staring back at her. Hadley impulsively pushed at it with her thumb, and was stunned when it popped out to the other side. She couldn't hear it fall to the ground. Instead, there was a rustling noise. At the same time, part of the gray sky lightened, like someone had lifted a dome partway.

"Who's there?" asked Hadley, looking into the opening. She saw only more gray, but now she heard breathing, loud breathing, as if through an amplifier.

"Whoever you are, you need to help me." Hadley braced her hands on either side of the hole and spoke through the opening. "Two old women have me trapped here. They say they're my aunts, but I don't think they are. I don't want to stay here anymore, but they won't let me go. There's no phone and no way out of the house."

Still no answer, but she could tell someone was there. How could someone be so cruel as to not respond? A warm gust of wind brought the scent of something sweet. She thought about it for a second and decided it smelled like a wintergreen breath mint.

"Please? I know you're there." Hadley felt her heart sink in dismay. The person had to be close. She tried again. "Can you call the police? My name is Hadley Brighton. Let them know I'm here."

More breathing, but no answer.

She pounded on the fence. "I'm stuck. Trapped. I need help!" Still no reply. She slammed her fists against the boards and yelled one long last word. "Help!" at the top of her lungs, but got nothing in response.

Off in the distance came a man's voice as loud as a crack of thunder. "Connor, my boy! Connor McAvoy, where are you?"

And then another voice, just as loud, this time coming from a boy. "Over here, Grandpa!"

In a panic, Hadley screamed out words that didn't sound like words even to her. She wailed, "Help me please," and "Don't go," and "Connor McAvoy!" all blended together in one awful sound. She was in a bad dream where nothing made sense and she had no power. Except it wasn't a dream. This was real, which made it the ultimate nightmare.

The sky above darkened once again into a dingy gray again, and there were no more sounds coming from the other side of the fence. Hadley rested her forehead against the rough wood and allowed herself to cry. Anyone would cry under these circumstances, she decided. She cried for a few minutes, and that was enough. She wasn't going to cry anymore.

Across the yard, Hadley heard the creak of the back door opening and Aunt Maxine's voice calling for her. The old woman yelled, "Hadley. Hadley child! Time to come in." A breeze swept away the scent of breath mine and the air now took on the damp, musty smell of a cellar.

Hadley called back, "In a minute." She wiped her eyes and smoothed the front of her shirt.

Aunt Maxine called her name again, this time more sharply, her voice getting closer. "Where are you, child?"

Hadley came forward. "Right here," she said, stepping out into the clearing.

CHAPTER 5

Aunt Maxine smiled in the way people do when they're very angry and trying not to show it. "What were you doing hiding in the trees?" she asked, gesturing with a tilt of her head.

"Just going for a walk to get some fresh air," Hadley said. "Stretching my legs."

"Just stretching your legs, hmm?" She towered over Hadley, casting a cold shadow. "And who were you yelling at?"

"No one."

"No one?"

"I was just randomly yelling things. I do that sometimes."

Aunt Maxine swooped in and grabbed Hadley's arm, her long fingers digging into the flesh. "Do you know what I do with liars?" she shrieked. The puffy sleeves of her dress rustled in the breeze, making her look even larger than she was.

Hadley struggled to talk. "I wasn't lying–" but she couldn't finish because she was being dragged across the yard with such force she couldn't get a foothold in the grass. "Please. Stop," she begged.

Abruptly Aunt Maxine halted in her tracks and lifted her so high that she dangled above the ground, her legs scrabbling in midair. "Ow, that hurts," Hadley cried.

"You think that hurts?" Aunt Maxine said. "You haven't seen the kind of pain I can inflict." She threw Hadley down to the ground so that she fell into a crumpled heap on the grass. "Here at Grimm House we do not disobey. We do not talk to strangers. We listen to our aunts. Do you understand?"

"Yes," Hadley said.

"Yes, what?"

"Yes, Aunt Maxine." She glanced up to see the silhouette of the woman blocking the light, leaving her in deepest shade. She and Aunt Charmaine each wore identical dresses every single day, a light blue frilly thing in a style more suited for babies than elderly women. It should have looked ridiculous, but on them it was frightening.

Aunt Maxine stuck her face close to Hadley's. "Repeat after me: Here at Grimm House, we do not disobey."

"Here at Grimm House, we do not disobey," Hadley said, gulping. She tried hard to keep her voice steady.

"You will not talk to strangers."

"I will not talk to strangers."

Aunt Maxine wagged a finger at her. "You will listen to your aunts."

"I will listen to my aunts."

"Is there something you want to add?"

"I'm sorry, Aunt Maxine. Really sorry."

"Not as sorry as you're going to be." Aunt Maxine smiled again, and this time it was the smug smile of satisfaction. She yanked on Hadley's hair and forced her to her feet. "Time for some well-deserved punishment." Still holding tight, Aunt Maxine marched her to the house.

Hadley, stumbling to keep up, murmured, "I'm sorry. I'm so sorry," as they went.

When they got to the house, Aunt Maxine pushed her through the open doorway. Hadley tripped and crumpled to the floor. As she got up, the woman gave her a shove and yelled, "Get your sorry self into the kitchen and sit down." She pulled a key ring out of her pocket and locked the back door from the inside.

Hadley did as she was told, pulling a kitchen chair away from the table and sitting down. She clutched her fists to her side and willed herself not to break down. *Do not cry! Do not cry*, she told herself. Her father had told her if she was ever lost to keep a calm head and trust her instincts. Her instincts said to get as far away as possible, but she wasn't going to be able to fight or run at the moment. Best to just get along and wait for a better opportunity.

Aunt Maxine came into the kitchen. When she lunged, Hadley reflexively drew back, expecting the worst, but instead of striking her, the old woman dragged Hadley, still in the chair, to the center of the room. "Let's take a good look at the little liar, shall we?" she said, going to turn on the overhead light.

Hadley blinked at the sudden brightness and smoothed down her disheveled hair. "I said I was sorry. I promise I won't be a problem again."

"Sorry?" Aunt Maxine threw her head back and laughed. "Sorry doesn't get the dishes done, girl. Sorry won't make you any taller or help you live longer. Sorry is nothing but a word and not even a good one. You'll have to do better than that."

"Of course, you're right. I'm sorry."

"There you go with the sorry again."

"I'm sorry. I mean—" Hadley clapped a hand over her mouth. "I take it back. I won't say it anymore."

Aunt Maxine paced back and forth, her long dress billowing behind her. In the light, Hadley could see every line and wrinkle on her face. She seemed to have gotten older in the last few days, and now age spots covered her hands and cheeks. Aunt Maxine stopped and poked a long, dirty fingernail at Hadley's chin. "You are not to leave this chair until I say so. Believe me, you could be sitting here all night." Up close Hadley got a whiff of a rank odor coming off Aunt Maxine. It smelled something like sour milk. "Do you understand me?"

"Yes, Aunt Maxine," Hadley said, trying to think of something, anything, besides what was happening to her now. She concentrated on the people who loved her most. Her mother and father. If her parents were here, they'd never let her be treated like this. They'd take one look and then scoop her up and take her home. Or at least that's how she imagined it.

When she was little and used to fall asleep in the car on the way home, her father would often carry her upstairs, and when they arrived at the apartment, her mother would get her ready for bed. Sometimes she'd stir slightly as they were tucking her in and kissing her good-night. When that happened, she knew she was loved. She was too big for her father to carry now, but she knew their love and their life together was real.

Aunt Maxine, not knowing that Hadley had managed the trick of imagining herself elsewhere, was busy ranting and raving. "In my day, children listened to their elders. None of this telling lies and not coming when they're called. The children today are horrible, dirty little things." She kicked at Hadley's grass-stained leg to make her point.

Hadley tried to shut her out with thoughts of her friends. Sophia, who danced like an angel. She dreamed of being a prima ballerina, but according to one of their teachers, Sophia didn't have the body type to dance professionally. She had been crushed at the news, but Hadley had hugged her afterward and said, "You can be the first then. The first with your body type to dance as a prima ballerina," and Sophia had wiped her tears and said, "Do you really think so?" And Hadley had said, "Of course."

And Lily, Hadley's biggest competitor. They had both done solos at the statewide competition last spring, and while they waited for the judges to decide, Lily had whispered in her ear, "I wish we could both win." Seeing Lily's face when they announced she was the winner took the sting out of losing. If it couldn't be her, she was glad it was Lily.

And all of her neighbors in the apartment building. She tried to call to mind the ones that mattered most to her. There were the doormen: Clyde, Phil, and Fred. Mrs. Knapp and her cute little dog, Chester. Mr. Mumbles, who never had much to say, but always held the door for her. Miss Kenny and Miss Goodman, who remembered her birthday and always came to her dance recitals.

Her life at home was grounded in people and things that she could count on. Fred, the doorman who always greeted her with a salute; the neighbors chatting about the weather; her friends sharing dreams of someday when all of them would be professional dancers. They would still be friends when they were grownups, they were all sure of that. She loved the predictability of it all. It was her life, and she loved her life.

At Grimm House, time passed unevenly, hours condensing and days stretched out like worms on the driveway after a spring rain. The aunts too, were odd, always wearing the same clothing but changing in other ways. When Aunt Maxine became angry or annoyed, her face turned crimson red. Both of the aunts had aged in the time she'd been here. She'd noticed more wrinkles and sagging skin. Suddenly Hadley realized something that made her sit up straight. "None of this is real," she blurted out.

"What did you just say?" Aunt Maxine stopped and gave her a hard stare.

"None of this is real," Hadley said. "I'm in a dream or hallucinating or something. It doesn't feel real."

"Not real?" Aunt Maxine crowed. "How can you say that?"

"Things here don't make sense, so they can't be real," Hadley said. "That's the only explanation. I'll wake up soon and be at home."

"I've got something that will help you wake up." Aunt Maxine sneered.

Hadley saw the woman's hand coming toward her and ducked but still felt the sting of a slap against her cheek. "Ow," she cried, pressing her hand to her face.

"I've had enough of your nonsense. You've officially lost your outside privileges. Get your butt upstairs until we call for you."

Hadley left the chair and ran up the stairs. When she got to her room, she curled up on the bed and pulled the scratchy blanket over her head. Breathe, she told herself, concentrating on nothing but inhaling and exhaling until she felt her racing heart slow down. Underneath the blanket, it was easy to imagine Grimm House was nothing but a bad dream. Nightmares didn't usually last this long, she knew, but anything was possible. Maybe when she woke up, she'd be back in her world again.

CHAPTER 6

Hadley awoke to the sound of labored breathing and the smell of someone long overdue for a shower. She opened one eye the tiniest bit and saw Aunt Charmaine sitting next to her on the bed. The old woman still wore the frilly light blue dress, but at this angle, Hadley now saw that the skin around her neck was puckered and loose. She squeezed her eyes shut and thought, *go away, go away, go away!*

A sharp finger jabbed at her rib cage. Poke. Poke. Poke. Hadley groaned.

"Are you awake?" The bed shifted as Aunt Charmaine leaned in toward her. There would be no getting away from her. "Hadley, dear? You've slept the whole day away. You need to get up."

Hadley sat up and rubbed the sleep out of her eyes. "What time is it?" A foolish question, as she hadn't seen a working clock in all the time she'd been in Grimm House. Lately it never seemed to be any particular time at all.

"It's time to get up, of course, you little dipsy doodle," Aunt Charmaine said, giving Hadley an awkward pat on the arm. Her gray springy curls bounced as she bobbed her head. "Maxine wanted to wake you up earlier, but I argued that we should let you get your rest."

"I was really tired," Hadley admitted, stretching her arms. "And now I'm hungry."

"Well of course you are!" Aunt Charmaine smiled down on her.

"Something smells good." Hadley said, turning her head toward the open doorway. "Turkey?"

"Not just turkey. A whole Thanksgiving dinner," Aunt Charmaine said. "Turkey, mashed potatoes and gravy, stuffing, yams, cranberries. The works!"

"Pumpkin pie, too?" Hadley's stomach rumbled.

"The best pumpkin pie you've ever had!" Aunt Charmaine stood up and clasped her hands together. "Topped with whipped cream. Or ice cream. Maybe both. Whatever you choose."

"But it's not Thanksgiving today," Hadley said, confused. "Or is it?"

"No, you big silly. It's not Thanksgiving. We're just celebrating."

Celebrating? Hadley jumped out of bed. That could only mean one thing. "They found my parents?" Happiness flooded through her. Soon she would be going home.

"Your parents? No. They haven't been found." Aunt Charmaine frowned. "I can't believe you're still fussing about those people. That was a long time ago." She picked at a piece of lint on the front of her dress. "Whatever made you think of them?"

"I thought that..." The lump in Hadley's throat kept her from finishing the sentence. Her eyes welled up with tears. She was afraid now she would never find out what happened to her parents. She couldn't imagine what it would be like to never see them again, never feel her parents' arms wrap around her in their cheesy group hug.

She could imagine how they looked sitting in the front row at her dance recital, her father calling her name as she made her bow. Both of them smiling, her mother blowing kisses her way. Love radiated off her mother and father like a sparkler giving off light.

Hadley had taken them for granted when they were still around. And now they were gone. Maybe forever, and she might never be able to tell them how much she loved and appreciated them. She looked over at Aunt Charmaine, who waited, mouth open, to hear the rest of what she had to say, but the words came out in a gargle of sounds. "Mmph my memm..." She choked a little and cleared her throat.

"Well, what is it? Spit it out, you little urchin." Aunt Charmaine put her hands on her hips. Her good mood had melted away.

Hadley gulped and worked to get out the words. "I miss my mom and dad."

Aunt Charmaine scoffed. "Oh for crying out loud. Wah. Wah. Wah. This is no time for blubbering." She grabbed Hadley's hand and pulled. "Come on. Wait until you see the feast I've prepared."

Down the staircase they went, Aunt Charmaine pulling Hadley behind her. The carpet on the stair treads was spongy and damp beneath her bare feet, making it hard to keep from sliding. Down another set of stairs, and when they got to the bottom, they just kept going, around the corner and down a long hallway. They ended up in the dining room, a dark paneled room with a long table covered with a linen tablecloth and set with fine china and tall candlesticks.

In the middle of the table, a golden roasted turkey sat on a platter next to a gravy boat, surrounded by serving dishes. The amount of food on the table could have fed a dozen people. The cranberries were topped with orange slices. Steam rose off the stuffing, and the mashed potatoes were whipped into a fine swirl. Aunt Charmaine steered her into the room. Hadley's mouth watered at the sight of the feast.

"Where do I sit?" Hadley asked, looking at the three place settings. She walked around the table, admiring the beautifully displayed food. The aroma alone could make a hungry person go mad.

Aunt Maxine appeared in the doorway, wagging a finger in her direction. "Not so fast. Dancing before eating."

Hadley took in a brave breath. After hearing Gigi talking about kids turning to ash, she'd decided not to dance for the aunts anymore. She didn't really understand it and wasn't sure she believed it, but it was the only thing she had control of. Why did Aunt Maxine and Aunt Charmaine insist upon it? Very odd. "I think I may have twisted my ankle. It really hurts," she said. "It wouldn't be a good idea to dance tonight. Maybe tomorrow," she added. Hopefully she'd find a way out of the house between now and then.

"You hurt your ankle?" Aunt Charmaine shrieked. "When did that happen?" She pulled out a chair and pushed Hadley down into a sitting position. She squatted on the floor and grabbed hold of Hadley's feet, turning them every which way.

Too late, Hadley remembered she should be reacting. "Ouch," she said, but it came out halfheartedly.

"Her ankles are fine," Aunt Maxine said firmly. "You will dance, Hadley, and you'll do it now, or you won't get any dinner."

"My dance teacher said you should never stress an injured ankle."

"Your dance teacher is an idiot. And so are you if you think I'm falling for this rubbish." Aunt Maxine pointed toward the parlor. "No more stalling. Get out there and dance." She sniffed in irritation.

Hadley got up and glanced sideways at the food. What would they do if she grabbed a spoon and took a quick bite? The two women were at least a million times older than her. Certainly she could outrun them. If she raced around the table, she might be able to taste almost everything.

"Don't be such a ninny," Aunt Charmaine said. "You know you love to dance, Hadley. Just do it and then we can all have a lovely meal together."

"I don't know where my dance shoes are," Hadley said. "I've misplaced them." She eyed the stuffing, just an arm's reach away. "I'll look for them later tonight and make sure I have them for tomorrow."

Aunt Maxine stepped in front of Hadley, blocking the view of the food. She leaned over and grabbed hold of her shoulders. They were so close their noses touched. "I am asking you one more time to dance. This is your last chance, so think carefully. There will be consequences."

Hadley stared into Aunt Maxine's bloodshot eyes and didn't blink.

Aunt Maxine said, "So will you be dancing for us?"

Hadley said, "No."

"You won't be eating anything until you do."

"That's okay. I'm not hungry."

"Really?" She raised one eyebrow. "Not hungry at all?"

Hadley's empty belly twisted in starvation. From the way it felt, she thought her stomach might have begun eating itself. Still, she held firm. "No. I couldn't eat a bite, thank you."

"Very well then," Aunt Maxine said, letting go. "You can sit there while we eat." She gestured to a chair in the corner of the room.

"I don't want to get in the way," Hadley said. "I'll just go clean up the kitchen." Before she could even take a step, Aunt Maxine's face flushed bright red. When she opened her mouth, a rush of foul air filled the room. "You. Will. Sit. Down," she shouted, her voice echoing off the walls. The sound scared every bit of bravery out of Hadley's body, and she found herself meekly taking a seat.

Aunt Maxine regarded Hadley coolly. "That's better. We don't stand for impertinence in this house."

Aunt Charmaine, who stood by with her arms crossed, said, "My sister has quite the temper, Hadley. It's not a good idea to defy her."

Hadley sat quietly, the tips of her toes brushing against the floral-pattern rug, while the aunts took their places at the table.

"Dark meat or light meat?" Maxine pointed at the turkey with the carving knife.

"Why not both?" Aunt Charmaine cried. She clapped as Maxine carved thin slices of the succulent meat and placed them on each plate.

Hadley gripped the sides of her chair when Aunt Charmaine loaded stuffing alongside the meat and doused both with gravy.

"I always think gravy makes everything better, don't you, sister?"

"Of course," Maxine said, scooping up a large dollop of mashed potatoes. "Just like butter on potatoes."

"Butter! I love when it gets all melty, like a little golden pond right in the middle," Aunt Charmaine said, sneaking a sideways glance at Hadley. "And don't forget the yams." She grinned. "Or the cranberries! I do love the cranberries."

They piled on the food until their plates were completely covered. Aunt Maxine made a point to look in Hadley's direction. "This is the best meal I've ever had. Easily the best. And I've had so many meals over the years."

"So delicious." Aunt Charmaine rubbed her midsection in an obvious way. "Every bite better than the next. We've really outdone ourselves this time." She groaned in delight.

Hadley tried to look away but found it nearly impossible. The aroma of the home-cooked meal assaulted her nose, and the sight made her salivate. Losing her mind was a distinct possibility. She tried to distract herself by thinking of other things. A plan, she needed a plan. Closing her eyes, she thought it through. Her goal was to escape from this house. Doors. Windows. The doors were locked, and the aunts kept the keys in their pockets. Pockets that were hidden in the folds of their dresses. Trying to reach the pocket would be like sneaking a key out of the crease of an accordion. Besides being locked, the windows were barricaded by strong metal bars that crisscrossed in a tight design. Too small for her to crawl through.

She would try the fence again tomorrow. And maybe, just maybe, Connor would send help. He had to have heard her. Just because nothing had happened yet didn't mean it wouldn't. She smiled at the possibility.

"Hadley!" A voice broke through her thoughts.

She opened her eyes. "Yes?"

Aunt Maxine, still at the table, held out a forkful of stuffing. "Are you sure you aren't hungry? There's so much food here, and it's so yummy. It would be a shame for you to miss out."

Hadley suspected a trick. "You'll let me eat without dancing?"

Aunt Maxine pulled the fork back and popped it into her mouth. "Oh no, you'd need to dance first, of course," she said, speaking with her mouth full. "That's nonnegotiable."

"Well then, no thank you."

Aunt Maxine shrugged. "Okay, have it your way."

CHAPTER 7

The meal went on for what seemed like hours, with the aunts exclaiming over each bite. They had second helpings of everything, and when they were through devouring every bit on their plates, they went straight for the pie. Hadley had never seen two people eat so much food. Aunt Charmaine put a large dollop of whipped cream on her slice of pumpkin pie and then stopped to admire it. "Doesn't the whipped cream look like soft-serve ice cream?" she asked Hadley.

Hadley nodded.

"This is easily the best pumpkin pie I've ever had in my entire life," Aunt Maxine said. "You've outdone yourself, Charmaine."

"Why thank you, sister. The trick is to sprinkle a bit of cinnamon sugar over the top right before you pop it into the oven. That's why it's so delicious."

"It is delicious. And creamy."

After dinner, the aunts allowed Hadley to leave her chair and join them in the parlor. "If you don't want to dance, perhaps just listening to some music would be lovely," Aunt Charmaine said. "You never know. You might change your mind." She went over to the Victrola, put a platter on the turntable, and turned the crank.

"Not tonight," Hadley said, leaning against the wall. "My ankle still hurts." She looked down at her bare feet, trying to remember if she'd specified which one was injured. "I think I might have broken a bone."

Aunt Maxine muttered, "If you want to be sure, I'd be happy to help you out and break one for you."

"Your ankles look fine to me," Aunt Charmaine said, dropping the needle onto the record. The room filled with soft music, and both aunts settled into their respective chairs. The space under the chandelier was open, waiting for a dancer's pirouette. As the music swelled, Hadley fought the urge to move to the center of the room. Every muscle in her body yearned to dance, but she folded her arms and tamped down the desire.

Aunt Maxine got up from her seat and stood under the chandelier. "Is this how you do it, Hadley?" she asked, holding her arms out and moving in a herky-jerky way. "Look at me. I'm Hadley. I can dance." She threw her head back and cackled.

Aunt Charmaine clapped enthusiastically. "All right, Maxine. Woo-hoo!"

The tempo of the music picked up, and Aunt Maxine spun in circles, her wide skirt spreading and lifting as she turned. The movement churned dust into the air, making Hadley's eyes sting. "I'm Hadley," Aunt Maxine screamed. "Look at me. Someday I will be on a stage, and thousands of people will clap for me."

"Go, sister, go!" Aunt Charmaine smothered a half-suppressed laugh.

"I'm Hadley," Aunt Maxine said. "And I dance and dance and dance because I am greedy for applause. That's why I practice so hard and take so many lessons. I want EVERYONE to love and adore me."

"She wants EVERYONE to love and adore her," Charmaine shrieked.

Aunt Maxine spun around and clasped a hand to her chest. "Love me. Adore me! I can dance."

"That's not right!" Hadley stepped away from the wall and shouted, "That's not right at all."

Aunt Maxine stopped mid-twirl to look at Hadley in wide-eyed amazement. "It speaks," she said.

"What, dear?" Aunt Charmaine got up and lifted the needle off the record. "What are you saying?"

Hadley felt like she'd been sleepwalking and had awoken to find herself with a clenched fist and a need to speak her mind. "That's not true. None of it's true! I don't dance to get applause, and I don't dance so people will love and adore me." Hadley thought of all the times she'd happily danced alone in her room. "I would dance even if I was the last person on Earth. I love to dance. I was born to dance."

Aunt Maxine sniffed. "So do it. Right here, right now." She pointed at the floor in front of her.

"No."

"Then I see no point in us having to look at your scroungy face any longer. Go up to your room right now. I don't want to see you until morning."

Hadley didn't move. "I want to know what really happened to my parents."

"Not this again," Aunt Charmaine said, groaning.

Hadley couldn't stop. She blurted out, "And where exactly am I? What is the address of this place? Why are you holding me prisoner here?"

"Dear Hadley," Aunt Maxine said, an edge to her voice. "I know you're going through a difficult time, but rest assured everything we do is for your own good. The world is a dark, scary place. You don't want to be out there, believe me. My sister and I are keeping you safe."

"Don't be such a ding-dong, little girl," Aunt Charmaine said. "It's not our fault something bad happened to your parents."

Hadley felt her lower lip start to tremble. "I want to go home."

"And I want you to dance," Aunt Maxine said. "But it looks like we're both out of luck for the time being."

"I need answers!" Even Hadley was surprised at how boldly she said the words. "I want to know what I'm doing here."

The prism in the room's chandelier dimmed and buzzed. Shadows on the walls swayed in a sickening way. Momentarily it felt like the whole house was dropping. Hadley grabbed on to the back of Aunt Charmaine's chair. When the movement stopped, the aunts exchanged a look Hadley didn't quite understand.

"That's enough, Hadley," Aunt Maxine said. "We're all tired, and it's time for bed. Go on up to your room and we can talk tomorrow."

Hadley left the room but lingered outside the doorway. She heard Aunt Charmaine say, "You should have had her stay to do the dishes. Now we'll have to do them ourselves."

Aunt Maxine said, "I couldn't risk her eating off the dirty plates. She needs to be good and hungry tomorrow."

"I've never seen such a stubborn child. The spell you put on her appears to be wearing off. I'm not sure she will dance, and we're running out of magic."

"Oh, she'll dance all right," Aunt Maxine said. "She's not going outside anymore, and she won't get another bite to eat until she does. You wait and see. Soon enough, she'll be begging to dance."

Aunt Charmaine chanted, "Not much longer and the passion will be ours!" Aunt Maxine joined her on the second round, and Hadley could still hear them singing as she reached the top of the stairs.

CHAPTER 8

A short while later, as Hadley lay in bed staring at the ceiling, she heard a knock on her door. "Hadley dear?" The door swung open and Aunt Charmaine's face popped into the opening. "Can we come in?"

Before she could answer, both of the aunts trooped into the room. She sat up, alarmed. "Did you want me to get up?" The light from the hallway startled her eyes.

"No, no, of course not, dear," Aunt Charmaine said. "Just relax." She circled around the bed and sat on one edge, then gestured to her sister to sit on the other side. Once Aunt Maxine took a seat, Hadley was trapped by the blanket stretched tight across her legs. "We just wanted to have a little talk with you. Isn't that right, Maxine?"

"Just a little talk," Aunt Maxine said with a twisted smile.

Aunt Charmaine said, "Things haven't been going so well, and we wanted to make it up to you."

"Okay," Hadley said craning her neck from side to side. With the aunts situated opposite each other, it was hard to know where to look.

"We may have gone a bit overboard," Aunt Charmaine said.

"Yes?" Hadley said eagerly, sure she knew where this was going.

Aunt Charmaine said. "We were perhaps a bit harsh. Don't you think, sister?"

"I'm not sure if I'd say harsh," Aunt Maxine said. "Compared to our childhood, Little Miss Dancer here has been treated like royalty."

"Sister!" Charmaine said. "Remember what we practiced." She spoke through clenched teeth. "Stick to the script."

Aunt Maxine sighed in an exaggerated way. "Hadley," she said, looking past Hadley toward the doorway. "We would like you to know that if we seem strict it is only because we are looking out for your best interests. We are your debated aunts." The words came out in a flat monotone. "What else? Oh yes. We care for you and love about you."

Aunt Charmaine held up a hand. "She means that we are your devoted aunts and that we love you and care about you."

Aunt Maxine harrumphed. "That's what I said!"

"No you didn't. You jumbled the whole thing up. After going over it so many times, you still couldn't get it right?"

"The little girl didn't know the difference." Aunt Maxine jabbed a finger close to Hadley's nose. "Look at her face. She's without a clue. An amoeba has more going on in its frontal lobe."

Hadley had heard enough. "An amoeba doesn't have a frontal lobe."

Aunt Charmaine spoke to her sister. "You'd better let me handle this." She patted Hadley's legs. "Hadley, dear. We know things aren't easy for you. You probably miss your parents. Most of the children do. And being in a strange place can require a bit of an adjustment." She glanced up at the ceiling as if trying to remember her lines. "And of course, not eating would make a child cranky. So we forgive you for not always being cooperative."

"How about *never* being cooperative," Aunt Maxine muttered under her breath.

"Sister!" Aunt Charmaine held a finger to her lips and then turned back to Hadley. "We wanted to let you know that you are forgiven."

"Okay," Hadley said. "Does that mean I can eat dinner?"

"Not tonight," Aunt Charmaine said. "But tomorrow night there will be plenty of leftovers available after you dance."

"But I thought..." Hadley hesitated. "I thought you were coming in to apologize and say I could eat."

"Apologize? You thought we were coming in to apologize? That's rich." Aunt Maxine scoffed and then addressed her sister. "What did I tell you? You bend over backwards for children, and they just think you're soft and try to take advantage." She flapped her hand and turned her head away like she couldn't stand to look at Hadley. "Ungrateful wretch."

"Oh, Maxine." Aunt Charmaine scooted in closer to Hadley. "She doesn't mean it, dear. She's just in a bad mood because she ate too much for dinner. Belly bog is what I call it."

Aunt Maxine said, "I hate it that you call it belly bog. That's a very crude term for a very real medical condition. I am suffering from what is officially known as intestinal expansitude. It's quite uncomfortable and nothing to take lightly. You could have some sympathy." Her stomach gurgled, and she patted it.

"Go ahead," Aunt Charmaine urged Hadley. "Tell her you're sorry for her suffering, and that will put things right between us."

"I'm supposed to say I'm sorry that she ate too much?" Hadley wondered aloud.

"That would be the kind thing to do."

"But she did it to herself!" Hadley said. "Besides, I'm starving. Why would I feel sorry for her?"

Aunt Maxine said, "It's no use, Charmaine. The child lacks even the smallest shred of human decency. She just doesn't get it."

"Shhh." Aunt Charmaine put an arm around Hadley's shoulder. "Every family has issues, but I think we've just had a very illuminating talk. Come on, Maxine, time to get in on a togetherness hug." Aunt Maxine's lips twitched, and for a second Hadley thought she would refuse, but then she leaned in. Right in between the two sisters, Hadley was encased in a cage of steely intertwined arms. Nothing like the warm and loving Brighton family group hug she shared with her parents. This hug smelled like a dirty laundry hamper and felt like being embraced by the monkey bars at the playground.

Aunt Charmaine pulled away and stroked Hadley's hair. "Now aren't you glad we came to see you before you fell asleep? I'm so glad we had such a lovely talk and worked things out. Tomorrow will be better. I'm sure of it."

"I hope so," Hadley said.

The aunts got up and Hadley felt the rush of blood flowing back through her legs. Aunt Maxine left the room first, and Aunt Charmaine paused at the door. "Good-night, sweet girl. We'll see you in the morning."

"Good-night." And then the door closed, and she was in the dark once more.

CHAPTER 9

That night after Hadley was sure the aunts had gone to bed, she stuck her pillow under her sheets and rearranged the blankets to make it look like a girl-sized lump. Stepping back, she assessed her handiwork. Not too bad. At a glance, even she could believe someone was sleeping underneath it all.

She went to the window and gave it one final try. It was locked, of course. And not a simple latch either; this required a key. On the other side of the glass, the window was covered with metal bars.

Even if she broke the glass, there wouldn't be enough space to crawl through.

Hadley went to the door and held her breath as she turned the knob and pulled the door open. Slowly, slowly, slowly. She stopped and listened. From down the hall, she heard the sounds of the aunts sleeping. Even through their closed doors, the snores came through loud and clear. Aunt Maxine vibrated like a freight train while Aunt Charmaine's nighttime breathing was high-pitched with an added whistle when she exhaled. Hadley closed the door behind her, then eased her way down the hall and down the stairs.

On the first floor, Hadley went from room to room, moving as quietly as a ballerina. The house was dark, but she felt her way around, checking each window and both the front and back door in turn. Just as she suspected, each was locked tight. And just like the windows upstairs, the decorative metal made it impossible to get through, even if she were able to break the glass. Grimm House was built like a fortress. Finally she gave up and went to the kitchen where she searched for food. The ice box had a padlock on it. That was new. The pantry closet had a padlock as well. The other cabinets and drawers held dishes and plates and cooking utensils but nothing to eat. She felt around in one drawer and thought she found a breath mint, but when she popped it in her mouth, it was something else entirely. Disgusted, she spit it into the sink.

Looking out through the window, the world was dark gray like a giant bowl covered the house. No moonlight, no stars, no streetlights. There were noises though: a faint mechanical clanking and the hiss of what sounded like a giant tea kettle. Hadley tried to figure out why it sounded familiar, but a second later it was quiet, and she wondered if she'd imagined it.

She leaned on the edge of the sink, so hungry she thought she could eat her own hand, when she heard it again. Outside. A hiss followed by some clanking. It was hard to tell where it was coming from. It seemed to be all around her. "What in the world?" she whispered to herself.

"Can't sleep?" A soft voice came from the counter next to her. Her heart jolted for just a moment until she spotted the glowing green eyes and realized it was the bug she'd met by the dustbin. The bug said, "It's me, Gigi. From the basement, remember?"

"I remember," Hadley said softly. "But you need to go away. I can't be talking to you now. Our voices might wake them up." She motioned in the direction of the stairwell.

"Suit yourself," Gigi said. "I just thought you might be hungry. If that's the case, I can be of some assistance."

"I am starving," Hadley admitted. "Do you know how to get the ice box open?"

"No, but I have something almost as good. Maybe better." Gigi let out a faint whistle and Hadley heard the sound of a thousand bugs scurrying along the floor into the room. The glowing eyes lit up the place making it nearly as light as day. She watched in amazement as a turkey leg was transported across the floor, stopping right at her feet. "For me?" she asked.

Gigi said, "Of course. We saved it for you before they cleared the table."

"And they didn't notice it was gone?" Hadley couldn't believe her luck.

"Nah."

She leaned over and grabbed the turkey leg. "Thank you," she said, putting it right to her lips and taking a big bite.

The sound of a thousand bugs chittered in response, their combined voices no louder than a kitten's sneeze. "You're welcome. Welcome! Welcome! No trouble at all!"

"There was another piece of turkey," Gigi said apologetically, "but a few of the younger ones didn't understand the concept of sharing." She glared down at the crowd on the floor. One of the little ones called out, "Sorry!"

"It's okay," Hadley said, her mouth full. "This will be enough." The outer layer of the turkey leg was crispy, the inside tender and juicy. She couldn't believe how good it was. Even if the aunts discovered her now, it would be worth whatever punishment they gave her. Every bite was more delicious than the last. She savored each mouthful, and when the meat was finished, she gnawed at the bone. How many times in the past had she left bits of meat stuck to a bone? Too many. She would never be so wasteful again. "What should I do with this?" she asked, holding what remained.

"Toss it down," Gigi said. "We'll take care of it."

Hadley dropped the bone, but it never hit the floor. Instead it was caught by members of the waiting throng. The group scurried out of the room with it perched on their backs.

"Thank you," Hadley said, wiping her hands on a dish towel. "Thank you so much. I thought I was going to die of starvation."

"I told you we could be your best friends in this house. Roaches get a bad reputation, but I'm here to tell you that we're not going away. Ever." Gigi reared up and motioned with her front legs. "We're fast and smart and indestructible. We're almost impossible to get rid of, so I don't know why people keep trying. They should just accept us the way we accept them."

With her stomach full of turkey, and the opportunity for a friendly talk, Hadley had a new appreciation for bugs. "Your name is Gigi?" she said, remembering the conversation in the basement. "Is that French?"

The bugs on the floor twittered in amusement. "French? Ooh la la. *Oui oui monsieur!*"

"It's not French?" Hadley said, picking up on their bug sarcasm.

Below her the bugs chattered some more. "*Parlez-vous français*? Ha-ha!"

"Not French. It stands for G.G.—green glowing eyes. See?" Gigi gestured to her eyes and made them brighten. "I can turn them on whenever I want. Pretty cool, huh?"

"I guess." Hadley leaned down so that she was nearly at eye level. "Can you help me get out of this house? Do you know how to unlock the doors or get through a window?" At her feet, the roaches created a carpet of glowing green eyes. When they moved, the glints of light speckled like sunlight on ocean waves.

Gigi shook her head. "Sorry."

"Can you maybe sneak out and go for help? There's this boy Connor who must be nearby, I heard him in the backyard—"

"There's no one outside who can help," Gigi interrupted.

"No, I heard him," Hadley said. "I mean, I heard his grandfather calling him."

"Just because you heard him doesn't mean he can help you. Believe me, that's not your way out."

"How can you be so sure?" Hadley asked.

Gigi scuttled closer. "This house stands alone. Except for us roaches, there's no one who can hear you."

Crestfallen, Hadley said, "So you won't help me?"

"I did help you. I gave you the turkey leg, didn't I? Now you need to help yourself," Gigi said. "It's like dancing. Do you ever get someone else to learn your routine and do your solos for you?"

"No, I would never do that."

"Well this is the same thing. It won't work unless you do it yourself."

"Do *what* myself?" Hadley felt her frustration swell.

Instead of responding to her question, Gigi said, "Did you go up to the attic yet?"

"No."

"Well, what are you waiting for? I told you the answers were up there."

Hadley didn't answer. Even thinking about going up in the attic frightened her to the core. What had Aunt Maxine said? That if Hadley went into the attic it would be the end of her. The end. No more Hadley. She tried to imagine not existing anymore. Her parents would never know what had happened to her. They'd be devastated to lose their only child. Without her, there would be no Brighton family group hug.

And what about her friends? Sophia and Lily would grow up and become professional dancers without her. She'd never get old enough to drive or have a boyfriend or know what it was like to graduate from high school. Even thinking about it made her horribly sad. She sniffed back what could turn into a fit of crying if she wasn't careful.

"So," Gigi said, her antennae twitching. "Are you going up there or not? I'm telling you it's the only way."

"Can't you just tell me what I'll find there?"

"No."

"Why not?"

"Because even as awesome as roaches are, we do have our limits," Gigi said. "This is something you need to do for yourself."

"Okay," Hadley said. "I'll do it. I'll go up to the attic."

"Great!" Gigi said. "Let's do it right now before you lose your nerve. We'll meet you up there." She leaned over the counter and let out a shrill whistle, and together the group of bugs on the floor arose in flight. They hovered in formation until Gigi zoomed in front of them.

"You can fly?" Hadley said, astounded, but there was no answer, just the sight of two thousand green glowing eyes flying out of the room with Gigi leading the way.

CHAPTER 10

After Gigi and the others left, Hadley had to wait until her eyes adjusted to the dark again. She walked out of the kitchen and through the dining room, pausing to look at the table, but there was no sign of the feast that had been there earlier. She continued on down the hall and was almost past the parlor, when she stopped.

The parlor. The only room in the house where she'd been truly happy, but that was only because she'd been dancing. After hearing what Gigi had to say, she was determined not to make that mistake again. Still, something pulled her to the center of the room, to the space under the chandelier where she'd danced blissfully until exhausted. She stood in the doorway, looking into the room, and wondered what it would feel like to stand in that spot one more time.

Hadley felt herself pulled to the center, stopping just beneath the chandelier. She glanced up, remembering how the light had lessened and buzzed when she'd spoken up for herself. A weird coincidence? Nothing made sense anymore, including the fact she was standing there. What was she doing? The aunts could wake up at any moment and discover that she was out of bed. This was no time to pause.

And yet she couldn't help herself. Just one minute couldn't hurt, could it? She closed her eyes and went into first position, heels together, feet facing outward, arms extended. She'd learned the five ballet positions at her very first dance lesson, and by now had done them hundreds, maybe thousands of times. It came as naturally as walking. Eyes still shut, she went into second position and held it for a moment before transitioning to third.

She could imagine her teacher, Miss Lavinia, walking through the line of girls, correcting the angle of an arm, reminding them to keep their heads high, telling them to hold the position.

Oh, she missed her life, every bit of it. She missed Sophia and Lily, dance lessons, and waking up in her own bed. She missed the sun on her face and greeting the neighbors on the elevator and laughing so hard she couldn't breathe. Most of all though she missed her mom and dad. If she just kept her eyes closed, she could pretend she was practicing at home. For just a moment, she'd be back where she belonged.

She continued, and when she got to fourth position, she sensed the light of the chandelier and opened her eyes in shock. What the heck? How did that happen? She looked around the room, but no one else was there. And then she noticed something she hadn't before. There was no light switch. How was the chandelier activated? She went to check for a switch outside the doorway, and the light dimmed to darkness. It was almost as if...

Thoughts whirred inside her brain. Had the light been on when she'd danced for the aunts before? It must have been, but she couldn't remember.

She tried an experiment, stepping directly underneath the chandelier and going through all five positions, this time with her eyes open. The chandelier came on, slowly at first and faint as a lightning bug. By the time she'd gotten to the fifth position, it was strong enough for her to see the flowers on the wallpaper. She stopped, and the light stayed steady for a minute or so and then faltered. A minute or two after that, it was out.

Was it possible that she was powering the light? She thought back to the times she'd danced for Aunt Maxine and Aunt Charmaine. It was always light in the room, still early evening at the start, so when the chandelier came on she wouldn't have noticed it. And then, when she was finished, they sent her up to bed so she wasn't around to see it when it went off.

But why? Why would two old ladies trap a girl in their creepy old house and then have her dance to power their chandelier? Why not just pay the electric bill like everyone else? Nothing in this house added up.

Maybe Gigi was right and the answers were in the attic. There was only one way to find out.

CHAPTER 11

When Hadley snuck out of her room and peered down the hall, she was surprised to see a light coming from an open bedroom door. Was one of them awake? No, the sounds she associated with the aunts' sleeping came through clear enough. Aunt Maxine's snore was as loud as a tuba. Aunt Charmaine inhaled with the hiss of a snake and exhaled in a thin whistle. Hadley left her room and eased her way out into the hallway, pausing between snores and moving along with the sound.

When she got to Aunt Charmaine's open door, she peered around the edge of the door frame, ready to run back to her room if she were caught. But there was no need for that. Aunt Charmaine was propped up in bed, her eyes closed and an open book lying across her chest. Her corkscrew curls were splayed out over the pillow. The nightstand lamp cast weird shadows in the room.

Hadley paused for a moment and took in the scene. Aunt Charmaine's room was much nicer than hers, with white furniture edged in gold. An oval mirror over the dresser was topped by two cherubs blowing kisses down to whoever would look into the mirror. At the ceiling, sculpted crown molding depicted familiar images. Hadley squinted, and did a double take of recognition. The crown molding showed birds and flowers similar to those in her room. She took a tentative step into the room to get closer, glancing at the sleeping woman who didn't stir. The flowers and birds weren't just similar to those in her bedroom at home. They were *exactly* like hers. She scanned the molding until she found the hummingbird. It was the same, right down to the raised wing. She remembered when her father had let her run her fingers over the sculpted feathers and told her that it was one of a kind. He'd certainly been wrong about that. The artist had done at least one more just like it, and here it was.

Her thoughts were interrupted by the creaking of the bed springs as Aunt Charmaine shifted in her sleep. The movement caused the book to slide off her chest and now Hadley could read the title: *The Beginners Guide to Immortality*. Aunt Charmaine mumbled in her sleep, "The prettiest thing he ever saw..." Slowly and carefully, Hadley backed away. Her heart thumping loudly, she crept out of the room and down to the end of the hallway.

Hadley opened the attic door, relieved to find it unlocked, and slipped through to the other side. Now she was in complete darkness. She paused for a second, then stuck out her hand to feel for the stairs. She found them, took a step up, and then stopped. All around her, it was black as new asphalt. She held her fingers in front of her face and couldn't see them. Maybe this wasn't such a good idea. What if something even worse than the aunts was hiding up there? Some kind of monster that fed on children? Oh, why did she think roaches could be trusted?

She stood there, paralyzed by fear and indecision, not wanting to go forward but not wanting to go back either. Out of the darkness came a voice, one she recognized. "So are you coming up or not?" Gigi asked.

"I can't see anything," Hadley whispered. "Is there a light?"

"No, but this might help."

Hadley blinked as the glowing eyes of a thousand bugs lit up in front of her, lining the walls on either side. "That's better," she said, climbing the stairs. The bugs moved with her, making an archway of light to guide her forward. When she turned the corner at the top landing, they zoomed ahead, flying up to line the ceiling of the open attic space.

For an attic, it was somewhat tidy. Rows of chairs lined each side of the room. On each chair was a suitcase or bag, and above the chair, photos were tacked to the wall. "What is all this?" she asked.

"Go ahead and see," Gigi said, encouragingly. She was perched on the top of the first chair, the one that held a brown suitcase with white stitching around the edges. On top of the suitcase was a saxophone.

Hadley pushed forward, ignoring the chatter of the bugs, who were cheering her on. "Not helping," she whispered, and they stopped.

She walked the length of the attic and noticed that each suitcase had something on top of it: a saxophone, a harmonica, tap shoes, juggling clubs, a magic show kit, sheet music, a notebook. Each photo showed a child about her age, labeled with a name. Enrico, Mary, John Paul, Amaya, Milton, Tracy, Derek. At the end of the row stood a single empty chair. Her photo was tacked above it.

"That's me," she said, jabbing a finger at the picture.

"Correct," Gigi said.

The other roaches chittered in unison. "It's a picture of Hadley! Hadley. Hadley. Hadley."

She held out a hand to make them stop and turned to Gigi. "What is all this stuff? What does it all mean?"

"These are all the children who've been in Grimm House, and these were their passions. If the aunts get their way, your suitcase will end up on the chair with your dance shoes on top of it."

"Really," Hadley said. She was beginning to think nothing in this house would surprise her anymore. She walked up and down the row of photos and stopped to study Enrico's face. Such a nice-looking boy. He was the one who'd had the saxophone. "What happened to all of them?"

"The two old women sucked their passion from them. That is how they can live forever. Passion energizes them."

"So the kids...they're dead?" Hadley asked, swallowing a lump of fear. "The aunts killed them?"

"Not dead." Gigi gestured with her front legs. "But they might as well be. Without passion, life has no meaning."

Hadley walked to the other side of the attic to study the names and faces above the suitcases. These photos were in black and white. The names were older: Abner, Cora, Pearl, Herbert, Bertha, Ethel, Nicholas. She turned back to Gigi and whispered, "I don't understand. If you knew all this, why didn't you just tell me? What was the point of me coming up here?"

Gigi zoomed past Hadley's face before landing on the top of a chair nearby. "Only one child came close to figuring it out, and that boy was a writer." She tapped her front legs together and twittered in glee. "I have to tell you that roaches can do almost anything. We can pass through walls and survive underwater for long periods of time. My kind can live without food for a month. And don't get me started on how well we can spread germs and bacteria. Oh boy, we excel in that area! I'm rather proud of that talent, if you must know."

"Is there a point here?" Hadley said, impatiently.

"Oh yes," Gigi said. "The point is that there is one thing roaches can't do, and that is read. The boy who was a writer was a smart one. From what I remember, he came close to figuring it out, but in the end they got his passion as well. I am thinking though that there must be something in that notebook that will help you." Gigi took off and hovered over the notebook.

Hadley picked it up and blew the dust off the brown leather cover. This was no grade school notebook. The cover was embossed with vines around the edges and stamped with his name: Nicholas.

"Read it, read it, read it," chattered the roaches from overhead. "Read it!"

Hadley had almost forgotten they were above her, lining the ceiling, keeping the lights on for her. "Shhh," she said. She set Nicholas's suitcase on the floor, sat on the chair, and opened the notebook. Inside the front cover it said, "To our wonderful son, Nick, on his tenth birthday. Love, Mother and Father." The date below showed that the notebook was given to Nick more than sixty years earlier. She turned to the first page and began to read.

At first she was just looking at the words, but as she got lost in Nicholas's story, she soon forgot about the stale, dry attic air and the green glow of the roaches above her. She carefully read each page, feeling better about her situation as she went. Just knowing that another child had experienced what she'd been through made her feel less alone.

When she finished the last page and closed the notebook, the roaches twittered in excitement. "She's done! She's done! Hadley finished reading!" Above her head, the ceiling lights shifted, creating a twinkling effect. "Good job, Hadley!" It took so little to make roaches happy.

She let the notebook rest on her lap and pursed her lips in thought.

"So?" Gigi said, hovering right in front of her face. "Was there something in there that will help?"

"Yes," Hadley said with a thoughtful nod. "There was."

CHAPTER 12

Hadley had left everything in the attic just as she'd found it and snuck back into bed. Sleeping wasn't an option. Her racing mind kept her awake. Nicholas's notebook was helpful and sad and funny. She found out that he did not mind being called Nicholas, but he really preferred Nick. He hated being called Nicky. He was thin and tall for his age, with dark eyes and curly hair. He had a small brown dog with triangle ears named Dash who loved him best of anyone in the world. Nick's father published the local paper, and very often Nick and Dash went to work with him during school breaks. Like Hadley, he was an only child. His father owned Hadley's apartment building, Graham Place, and they lived on the top floor.

Nick had also been whisked away by the aunts when his parents were away—his mother sick in the hospital and his father at her bedside. He wouldn't be allowed to visit his mother at the hospital until her fever went down, he'd written. Just like Hadley, he found himself in Grimm House with the aunts who weren't really his aunts, and just like Hadley, they encouraged him to do his passion every evening in the parlor.

In Nicholas's case, his passion had been writing. Poetry, in particular. Hadley didn't think his poems were very good. In fact, she rolled her eyes at some of the rhyming. But she'd give him credit for being clear and concise. She also gave him credit for figuring out a way to get information out of the aunts.

Instead of demanding answers, Nick had used another strategy. "I am disarming them with kindness," he wrote. "It will buy me time to figure out how to escape, and their guard will be down."

He was able to write these notes, he said, because they never looked at his notebook but instead had Nick read his poems aloud.

> *Aunt Maxine*
> *With eyesight so keen*
> *A voice so commanding*
> *I find it demanding*
> *I ask if I may*
> *Her rules I obey*

Aunt Maxine did not care for this poem, Nick said. He wrote that her eyebrows, "Knit into a V, and her lips made one thin, straight line." The next poem, the one about Aunt Charmaine, was received somewhat differently.

> *Aunt Charmaine*
> *She sings like a bird*
> *And knows every word*
> *Her voice is so lovely*
> *Surely she loves me*
> *Aunt Charmaine*
> *Is very pretty*
> *Smart and warm*
> *And funny and witty*

It was this poem that helped Nick come to the realization that, of the two sisters, Charmaine was the one most likely to help him. She adored this poem and had him recite it several times until Aunt Maxine had snapped, "Enough, Charmaine! He needs to be writing new poems, not just repeating the same one over and over again."

After that, Charmaine had waited until Maxine wasn't around and asked him to recite it a few more times. She blushed as he said the poem and smiled the entire time. Nick wrote that she twirled a piece of hair around her finger like a schoolgirl.

Nick wrote, "It is as if Aunt Charmaine never heard anyone say something nice about her. She lives in her sister's shadow and is pleased with even the smallest compliment."

Hadley's eyes had widened when reading that. Nick was a clever boy. It had never occurred to her to try being extra nice to the two sisters. The rest of the notebook was filled with poems about gardens and butterflies and starry skies, but the notes Nick wrote about Grimm House told the real story. Because of that poem, he was able to win Aunt Charmaine's confidence. Every time he recited it, he'd get her to tell him a little more until finally he knew the truth of Grimm House.

"There have been other children here over the years," he wrote. "All of them originally from Graham Place. Aunt Charmaine says she and her sister spirit them away when given the opportunity, but only when necessary." In the margin he had scribbled, "Whatever that means," with an arrow pointing to the word "necessary."

He went on to explain that all of the children had different talents, what the aunts called passions. Aunt Charmaine seemed to think that robbing the children of their passions was doing them a favor. She'd said, "Children can become too obsessed with doing one thing all the time. If we take it away from them, it's like we've lifted a curse."

Nick pretended to agree in order to get more information. "She said that after a few performances, the child's passion gets drawn up into the chandelier, and once that happens, it keeps everything going for years and years," he wrote. "The chandelier is the life source for all of Grimm House, not just the aunts. It's important to them that the chandelier is safeguarded and remains untouched." He jotted a note on the edge of the page: "How to reach it? Look for ladder or stepstool."

Time worked differently in Grimm House, Nick wrote. What seemed like weeks were actually minutes. As their power weakened, time and energy slipped away from them. *Hmm*, Hadley thought. No wonder she couldn't get a good grasp of how long she'd been there. Originally she'd tried to keep track of the days here, but after a little while it all became a muddle and she'd given up. She kept reading.

The aunts' magic came from the chandelier, but by the time they needed a child's passion, it was nearly depleted and they were in danger of fading away entirely. "We can keep the house running and arrange for food to be delivered," Aunt Charmaine said, "but even that only lasts so long. We need the passion to keep going." Passion was their life blood, the thing that fueled them, the means for them to go on forever. "And doesn't everyone want to live forever?" she'd said.

Aunt Charmaine had told Nick that once a child's passion was removed, they were returned to their home and didn't have any memory of being at Grimm House. "And since almost no time has passed at all, they haven't lost anything," she exclaimed.

"But I won't be able to write poetry anymore?" Nick had asked.

"Well no," Aunt Charmaine had said with a wave of her hand. "But really, how many people write poetry anyway? It's a dying art form. And think of all the time you'll gain that you would have wasted scribbling away in that notebook. You'll see. It'll work out fine. Your parents will think you outgrew the notion, and you won't know the difference."

Nick had pretended to agree with her, but secretly he was sickened by the idea. In the notebook, he wondered: "Will I be the same person if I can't put my thoughts down in words? Will my life be the same without my poetry?"

He didn't have an answer, but Hadley did. "No," she whispered later, alone in her bed. No, Nick would not be the same person or have the same life without his poetry. She knew this because her life without dancing would be incomplete. She read on, hoping that Nick had figured out a way to get away from the aunts, but she knew that wouldn't be the case. His suitcase and notebook were there along with all the other children's prized possessions. Enrico's saxophone. Mary's tap shoes. Milton's juggling clubs. All of their passions stolen by Grimm House and the aunts.

As the days went on, Nick got more and more lonely, aching to see his parents again. He was especially worried about his mother. The last time he'd seen her, she'd been ill with a high fever and a croupy cough. He wrote a long description of how she'd taken ill and crumpled to the floor. Right to the end, even with a high fever, she'd tried to take care of the family. Nick was tormented by the thought that she might be asking for him and he wasn't there. "I can't stand it any longer," he'd written. The last poem in the notebook spelled out Nick's decision:

Grimm House at night
Is a place like no other
I want my father
I miss my mother
Chandelier
Needs me near
I'll write this poem
To help me go home

His final poem, Hadley mused, and he had to go and mess up the rhyme by pairing poem with home. A sad ending to a sad story. She was pretty sure Nick went home without his passion. With his mother in the hospital, it might have been the right decision, but she didn't want her story to end the same way.

CHAPTER 13

The next day, Hadley put her plan into place. "Good morning, Aunt Maxine," she said as she entered the kitchen. "Good morning, Aunt Charmaine." She smiled widely, doing her best impression of a pleasant, well-mannered child.

"Well, aren't you a ray of sunshine," Aunt Charmaine said. She stirred whatever was in her mug and tapped the spoon on the side. "I hope you've learned your lesson, little miss." On the other side of the table, Aunt Maxine eyed her suspiciously.

"I have," Hadley said. "I have learned my lesson. I am truly sorry."

Aunt Charmaine nodded in approval. "You're forgiven."

"Not so fast," Aunt Maxine held up one bony finger. "You're not eating anything, not a crumb until after you dance. Do you understand?"

"Yes, Aunt Maxine."

"And you won't be dancing until this evening at the usual time."

"Yes, Aunt Maxine."

"And you are no longer permitted to go outdoors. Is that clear?"

"Yes, Aunt Maxine."

Aunt Charmaine gave Hadley a long look. "I must say I appreciate your cooperative spirit, Hadley. Are you planning on entertaining us with your dancing this evening?"

"Yes, Aunt Charmaine. I actually have a new routine I'm very excited about. You might even say..." Hadley said, pausing for effect, "...that I feel very passionate about it." The aunts exchanged an astonished look at the use of the word passionate. Hadley continued, "There's just one thing..."

"Yes?" Aunt Charmaine said.

"I was hoping to make this a really special performance, so I wanted to use some props and maybe rearrange the furniture so I have a different dance surface." Seeing the look on Aunt Maxine's face, she hurried to smooth things over. "You don't have to do a thing. I'll take care of it all just using things from the house."

"You aren't going to break anything?" Aunt Maxine asked.

"Oh no, Aunt Maxine. I'll be really careful. I promise! This is just to help me get into the performance. I'm feeling really passionate about this dance. I think it's going to be my best yet."

"I'm not so sure about this," Aunt Maxine said, scowling. "Why can't you just dance the way you usually do?"

Aunt Charmaine jumped in. "Oh, what's the harm, sister? I for one can't wait to see what the little simpleton has come up with. I'm sure it will be wonderful."

"Well, all right," Aunt Maxine said with great reluctance. "As long as I don't have to start moving furniture around. I'm not about to strain myself with your foolishness."

"You won't. I promise. I'll take care of everything." Both aunts were staring at her now, making it hard to hold her pleasant smile. "May I be excused to my room to go practice my dance routine?"

"You may," Aunt Charmaine said. As Hadley was leaving the room, she said to her sister, "Now that was a nice turnabout. See, you don't have to hang a child by their thumbs to get some cooperation."

Aunt Maxine said, "I find the whole thing fishy. Yesterday she refused to dance, and today she wants to use props and rearrange the furniture? I'll be glad when we're done with this girl. She's a weird one."

Hadley went to the front hall and unhooked the umbrella off the coat rack. Hanging on the wall behind it was Gigi, this time alone. Gigi said, "What's the story with the umbrella? Are you thinking you're going to fly out of here like Mary Poppins?" Without the rest of the roaches, Gigi looked small, her two glowing eyes like dots of a laser pointer.

"Shhh." Hadley looked behind her, but the aunts were nowhere in sight. "No, I'm not going to fly. It's a prop for my performance tonight."

"I don't get it," Gigi said. "What are you going to do?"

"I have a plan." Hadley slung the umbrella over her shoulder. "Wait and see."

When Hadley got to her room, she found three oatmeal cookies and an apple sitting on her bed. She guessed it was a gift from Gigi and company. Or maybe from Aunt Charmaine, going behind her sister's back? She took a bite of the apple, not caring where it came from, just enjoying the juicy crunch. She ate it all, even the core, and then went right to the cookies. Hadley chewed slowly to make them last longer. When she was finished, she slurped some water from the bathroom faucet until she felt full. It didn't make up for the meals she'd missed, but it was enough for now.

Hadley spent the rest of the day in her room, lying in her bed, staring at the ceiling. If her plan worked, would she immediately be returned to home, still a dancer? Or would her interference ruin everything, breaking the portal between here and her old life and forcing her to stay in Grimm House forever? It was this possibility that scared her the most, and there was no way of knowing for sure. If she thought about it too much, her heart sped up in terror and she considered backing down and going the same route Nick did. Doing what the aunts wanted was the only certain way to get back to her old life. It was tempting, except for the fact that she'd be forfeiting the one thing that made her who she truly was.

She dozed for a few hours and woke when Aunt Charmaine came into her room to let her know it was time. "You must have been practicing up a storm if you're so tired you fell asleep," she said.

"I was." Hadley rubbed her eyes. "Practicing a lot, I mean."

"Good for you." Aunt Charmaine picked up the umbrella. "Was it raining in here?"

"No. It's a prop for my performance."

Aunt Charmaine nodded approvingly. "How creative of you. I'm sure it will be charming."

"Is it time to dance?"

"Yes, indeed. Get your dance shoes on, girly girl," Aunt Charmaine said, "and go wait in the parlor. Maxine and I will be there directly."

After Charmaine left, Hadley pulled on her shoes, grabbed the umbrella, and went downstairs to wait. Soon Gigi appeared, chattering into her ear. "Is your plan something that was in that kid's notebook? Because it didn't turn out so well for him."

"I know. You don't need to remind me." Hadley set the umbrella down. From the kitchen, she heard the aunts squabbling and calling each other names.

"Shrew!"

"Harridan!"

"Hag!"

"Harpy!"

"Nag!"

"I'm a nag? If anything, you're the nag!"

They were laughing now, which meant she had to hurry to get everything in place before they arrived. She took the lamp off the library table and set it carefully on the floor, then scooted the table inch by inch to the center of the room. She glanced at the doorway, hoping the aunts wouldn't come in just yet. She strained as she moved it back and forth, trying not to make any noise.

"What's the story here?" Gigi asked, fluttering in front of her eyes. "You know you're putting it right underneath the chandelier?"

"No duh." Hadley swatted her away. "I'm using it as a stage."

"Huh." Gigi landed on the table, her antennae twitching. "Isn't the whole idea to get as far away from that thing as possible?" She gestured upward. "Seems to me like you're doing the opposite."

"You'd better go before they see you," Hadley whispered. She was nervous enough without having a roach put doubts in her mind.

Gigi said, "I'm just trying to help you out here. You don't have to be so grouchy."

Hadley started to say that she wasn't being grouchy, but Gigi had flown off before she could get the words out. Once the table was in place, she waited off to one side, ready to make a dramatic entrance.

"What's this?" Aunt Maxine said as the two aunts strode into the room. She pointed disapprovingly at the table now located dead center underneath the chandelier.

Hadley came running from the corner of the room, the umbrella under one arm. When she reached the table she gracefully hoisted herself up onto it and stood. "It's a surprise for you. A stage for dancing, so you can see my footwork more closely."

"Get down from there right now," Aunt Maxine said, irate. "You shouldn't be standing on the furniture!"

"You could fall and hurt yourself," Aunt Charmaine said.

"I won't fall," Hadley said. "I've been practicing all afternoon. I have this down."

Aunt Maxine swooped out a long arm to grab her leg, but Hadley leaped out of reach and spun around. The old woman tried again, just missing Hadley's hand.

"She is fast." Aunt Charmaine said, admiringly. "And she does seem to be a bit more spirited up there. Why don't we let her try?"

"Let her try?" Aunt Maxine repeated, her voice a screech. "And if she falls and breaks her neck, then what? The passion dies with her and we've just wasted our time." She stood with her head tilted back, watching as Hadley pirouetted and leaped.

Aunt Charmaine went to the Victrola and turned the crank. "Please, sister," she said. "I want to see her new routine." When she put the needle on the record and the music began, Aunt Maxine threw up her hands and went to her chair. Aunt Charmaine settled into her seat and said, "You'll see, Maxine. I have a good feeling about this. She's giving it her all. This might be Hadley's final curtain call."

Aunt Maxine said, "If you're not right, you'll wish you were."

Hadley made up some random moves involving the umbrella, wielding it with a flourish, then holding it with both hands and jumping over it.

"Yes!" Aunt Charmaine said, pumping her fist in the air. "Wonderful, Hadley."

Even Aunt Maxine looked somewhat enthused, clapping and tapping her foot to the music. "Nicely done," she said.

Above Hadley's head, the chandelier went from dark to dimly lit, buzzing with excitement. Hadley knew she couldn't wait too much longer to make her move. She distracted the aunts with a high kick followed by a triple spin with her leg extended. Aunt Charmaine clapped so hard it could be heard over the music. Aunt Maxine's mouth opened wide into an O of approval.

The chandelier crackled, anticipating Hadley's energy. Glancing upward, Hadley saw Gigi on the ceiling taking it all in. Any moment, she knew, her passion could be sucked away while her regret and longing would be left behind as a pile of ashes. And then she would be whisked back home, never remembering Grimm House or what had happened there, always wondering why she no longer had any talent or passion for dance. She felt a tug from above and knew it was now or never. Boldly she reached up with the curved handle of the umbrella and hooked it around the chandelier's chain and yanked. When it didn't give way, she lifted her legs so her entire weight was hanging off the light fixture. The chain started to yield. She dropped an inch and then another...

"What are you doing?" Aunt Charmaine cried out.

As Hadley swung from the chandelier, she caught sight of Aunt Maxine's face contorted in fury. "Enough!" she shouted, rising to her feet, her face turning red. The next thing Hadley remembered was the smack of Aunt Maxine's hand hitting her across the back and knocking her off the chandelier. She flew across the room and fell with a crash.

Her head hit the floor, and all went dark.

CHAPTER 14

A half hour later, Hadley blinked her way out of the darkness and saw Aunt Charmaine's face come into focus above her. "How did I get here?" she asked, looking around. She was lying on her back in her Grimm House bedroom with the old woman dabbing a wet washcloth on her forehead. Hadley's dance shoes were still on her feet, and she felt a definite lump on the back of her head, so yes, it had happened. She had actually swung from the chandelier, felt it yield to her weight, and gotten knocked to the floor by Aunt Maxine. She'd come close to breaking the chandelier's hold, but not close enough.

Aunt Charmaine clucked her tongue. "Oh Hadley, you little dunderhead. Do you have any idea what you've done?" She refolded the washcloth and pressed it first on Hadley's forehead and then her cheeks. This small kindness reminded Hadley of her mother, making her more homesick than ever. "Sister is furious. You've nearly spoiled everything. What were you thinking?"

Hadley sat up and made a quick decision. If Aunt Charmaine thought she was a dunderhead she would play the part. "She didn't like my dance routine?" She screwed up her face as if about to cry. "But I practiced and practiced, and I wanted so very much to please both of you." She held her hands together, fingers pointed upward. "Please forgive me."

"You stupid girl," Aunt Charmaine said. The words were harsh, but her tone was affectionate. "Did you really think hanging off the chandelier was a good idea? Where would you get such a thought?"

"I saw it in a movie once," Hadley said, making her lip tremble. "The audience in the movie loved it and gave the dancer a standing ovation. I thought you might love it too." She leaned forward, resting her head against Aunt Charmaine's ample front. She let out a few fake cries of anguish. Maybe not her best performance, but judging from the way Aunt Charmaine patted her back, it was working.

Aunt Charmaine said, "You nearly broke the chandelier! Luckily we stopped you in time and it still works."

"I'm sorry..." Hadley gulped and stammered. "I'm sorry that I let you down. I tried so hard." Oddly enough the words had an effect on Hadley; she felt her eyes fill with tears. "So very, very hard."

"Now, now." Aunt Charmaine heaved a heavy sigh, jostling Hadley's head. "Maxine wanted to be through with you, but I convinced her to give you one more chance."

"Oh, thank you!" Hadley pulled back and wiped her eyes. "You're the best, Aunt Charmaine! You're warm and funny and witty and kind." Aunt Charmaine looked confused. For a moment, Hadley thought she would recall that the words were from Nick's poem, but the moment passed without her making the connection.

"Well, yes," Aunt Charmaine said, agreeing with the compliment. "I did talk my sister into letting you dance one more time, but believe me, that will be it. If you pull something else, I can't even imagine what will happen. Maxine has a terrible temper."

"I know," Hadley said.

Aunt Charmaine hooked a finger under Hadley's chin to get her attention. Her gaze was intense. "You must dance, and when you do, you must give it your all. No tricks, nothing out of the ordinary. Do you understand?"

"I understand."

"Be a good girl, Hadley." Aunt Charmaine sat up straight. "This will be your last chance to get it right. If you don't dance, you'll be banished far, far away and wind up nowhere. And believe me, nowhere is not the place to be." She shuddered. "It's cold and empty and lonely and never ends." She gave Hadley's shoulder a gentle squeeze. "Got it?"

Hadley nodded. "Do you want me to dance for you now?"

She shook her head. "The time has passed, so it will have to be tomorrow. You'd better stay in your room until then. Just the sight of you might trigger an attack of apoplexy in my sister."

Hadley nodded. She didn't know what apoplexy was, but she knew she didn't want to experience it firsthand. "I'll stay right here until you call for me."

"Good girl." Aunt Charmaine got up off the bed. "I'll let Maxine know that you'll behave yourself tomorrow. Soon it will all be over, you'll see."

"Thank you." Hadley watched as the door closed and heard the soft click of it being locked from the other side. She got up and checked. Sure enough, Aunt Charmaine had locked her in, and there she would stay until her command performance tomorrow. Hadley went back to the bed, feeling the full weight of her sorrow. It was over. Soon she would be home, back in her own bedroom. Just a few more days with babysitter Zoe, and she'd be reunited with her parents.

She'd have her life back, but it would be diminished. Without dancing, what would she do with her free time? What activity could replace it? She woke every day dreaming of dancing and couldn't wait to get to it. Her friends were dance friends. The girls in her dance class were what her mother called "her people." The other girls all knew the triumph of mastering difficult dance steps, of making your body move in a precise, graceful manner. Hadley didn't want to give that up. She couldn't give that up. And yet she couldn't stay here any longer. She now knew firsthand what Nick had gone through, the difficult choice he'd had to make that had prompted his last poem.

Grimm House at night
Is a place like no other
I want my father
I miss my mother
Chandelier
Needs me near
I'll write this poem
To help me go home

She hugged her legs to her chest and moved her lips soundlessly. "Please. Please. Please. There must be a way to do both—go home and keep my passion for dance. If only I had a clue. If only someone would tell me what to do." She thought it through. The chandelier had been the key. That part Nick had gotten right. She'd been so sure her plan would work. Bring down the chandelier and you break its power. Seeing how quickly Aunt Maxine sprang to action confirmed how close she'd gotten. But the two aunts would never let her stand on a table again, much less with something like an umbrella.

And she hadn't come across a ladder or stepstool. It was hopeless.

Hadley knew she had to do what the aunts wanted. If she didn't, Aunt Charmaine had said she'd wind up nowhere. What would nowhere be like? She shivered, thinking of all the possibilities.

CHAPTER 15

Hadley pondered her predicament for hours. She tried to think about it in a logical, problem-solving way. The two aunts, who were not her aunts, were witches. That much was clear. They wanted something she could easily give, but she didn't want to give it to them. Letting them have her dancing spirit would take her home. The alternative was to wind up nowhere. She imagined nowhere as being like the room she was currently in but without furniture or the hope of leaving. Dreadful. She absolutely, positively didn't want to go nowhere.

She tried to envision a life without dance. Plenty of free time to do whatever she wanted. Entire weekends stretched before her to spend any way she desired. She could ride her bike. Learn to cook from her father. Take up skateboarding. Read books before they became movies.

All of those things sounded like fun. For someone else. But for her, it would be a second-best kind of life.

Hadley was dwelling on this thought when she saw an oatmeal cookie slide under the door, followed by another, both of them pushed by a cluster of glowing-eyed roaches. The cookie-pushing roaches were accompanied by hundreds more, all of whom swarmed into the room, fanning out around Hadley.

"For me?" she asked, getting off the bed and picking the cookies off the floor.

The group rose up on their hind legs and spoke in unison. "For you, Hadley! Cookies! Cookies for Hadley!" One of the little ones called out, "And I didn't eat any of it this time!"

"Thanks!" Hadley called down.

One of the roaches flew up and hovered near Hadley's face. Gigi. "You might want to blow on them," she said. "We encountered a little dust on the way."

Hadley pursed her lips and watched as dust rose off the cookie, then took a bite. "This is so good," she said, savoring the chewy goodness. "Thank you. I was really hungry." She polished off both cookies in short succession and finished to the muffled sounds of hundreds of roaches clapping their legs together. "Well done, Hadley! Hooray for Hadley!" She stood and bowed, then sat down again. "You've been so nice to me," she said. "I wish I could do something for you."

Gigi, who was perched on the pillow, wiggled her front legs. "That's a nice thought, but really, what could you do for us? You're just a girl. We're roaches, superior in every way. We can hide in an instant. Mobilize in a second. Band together or work on our own." Gigi sounded gleeful. "That's true of all roaches, but we're a special kind, newly evolved. Better in every way."

"You sure brag a lot," Hadley said.

"You'd brag too if you could do what I can do." Gigi's eyes glowed brighter. "We can squeeze through tiny cracks and crevices and move from room to room without detection. We would make wonderful thieves. How do you think we got the cookies without the old ladies seeing?"

"I'm really glad about the cookies," Hadley admitted. "It's true that I can't squeeze into tiny cracks, but I am bigger than you and my brain is larger too."

"Your bigger brain hasn't seemed to help you much in this predicament, has it?"

"No," she said sadly.

Gigi shook her antennae. "Don't feel bad. You can't help being a human."

"And you can't help being a bug." Hadley scooted back on the bed and crossed her legs.

"Hey!" Gigi said. "Don't say it like that. I wouldn't trade being a roach for anything."

"Really?" Hadley couldn't imagine wanting to be a bug if you could be something else. Anything else.

"Really." Gigi scurried to the edge of the bed and called down to the crowd below. "I'm taking a vote. Who loves being a roach?"

The throng of roaches roaring in agreement was as loud as the shuffling of many papers. "Roaches rule! Yay for roaches."

Gigi waved an arm and the group stopped at once. "See? We have all the advantages of being a single bug *and* being a group. When we're together, we are as strong as a gorilla."

"A gorilla, huh?" Hadley picked at an oatmeal crumb on the front of her shirt and popped it into her mouth.

"Absolutely," Gigi said, getting more excited as she spoke. "We carry our body armor with us and can lift incredibly heavy loads. Really, there's nothing that's better than being a roach. We can do anything. You know they say that when the world ends and all the humans are gone, we'll still be around."

The world ending. Not a very cheery thought, but Hadley didn't stop to reflect on it because an idea had popped into her head. "How many of you roaches are there?" she asked.

"Millions!" Gigi said.

"No, I mean, here. In Grimm House."

"Millions, give or take," Gigi said. "There are always new ones, so it's hard to take attendance."

"Millions right here in Grimm House?" Hadley asked incredulously. "Why haven't I seen that many?"

"Because we are experts at subterfuge, masters of camouflage, professionals at blending in!" Gigi chirped. "We're only seen when we want to be seen.

You've been lucky that way, getting to see us. Not everyone does."

"You get to see us!" chirped some of the smaller ones from the floor.

Hadley smiled down and gave a quick wave before asking Gigi, "You say roaches can do anything?"

"Anything and everything!" Gigi spoke to the masses below. "Isn't that so?"

The roaches on the floor chimed in. "Anything. Everything! Whatever we want." And then they rolled on the floor laughing in the way only roaches can.

"Everything that matters," Gigi added. "And some things that don't."

"I've got a project for you," Hadley said. "It's something that matters."

CHAPTER 16

Hadley had to admit that Gigi had been right—the roaches did turn out to be her best friends at Grimm House. They eagerly embraced her new idea, even after she explained that their involvement in the scheme might put them in danger. "We don't mind. We don't mind!" the younger ones clamored until finally Gigi told them to shush.

"We all have to work in perfect synchronicity or it won't work," Gigi said. They spent the next few hours practicing a modified version of the plan. It worked out even better than Hadley had hoped.

When the aunts trooped up the stairs at bedtime, Hadley and the roaches had just finished their last practice. At the sound of someone approaching the door, Hadley froze in place next to the bed. When she heard a key in the lock and the door swung open, every roach in the room magically disappeared. It happened so quickly she could have been convinced she only imagined them.

Aunt Charmaine popped her head in the door. "Hadley? Would you like to use the bathroom before bedtime?"

She did, of course, and would have said yes even if she didn't. Aunt Charmaine stood guard out in the hallway while she used the toilet and washed her hands and face. In the reflection, Hadley took a good look at herself. Something had changed. The girl in the mirror was still her, just a more clever, more determined version of herself. This new Hadley could break rules if she had to. She smiled and silently mouthed the words, "I. Will. Win." After she dried her hands on the towel, she left the room and crossed the hall like the obedient child Aunt Charmaine believed her to be.

"Good-night, Hadley," she said, getting out her key. "See you tomorrow."

"You *will* see me tomorrow." Hadley sounded agreeable but the underlying meaning of the words tickled her fancy. The aunts would see her tomorrow. They thought what they'd see would be a helpless child who would bend to their will, but instead they would get something else entirely. "Good-night." Hadley pulled the door shut herself.

She slept well and dreamed for the first time since she'd arrived at Grimm House. In her dream, she was surrounded by other children. Somehow she knew they were the kids who'd lost their passions to the aunts: Enrico, Mary, John Paul, Amaya, Milton, Tracy, Derek, Abner, Cora, Pearl, Herbert, Bertha, Ethel, and Nicholas. It was a sunny day in her dream, and all of the children were playing in the park. Their clothing was from different time periods, like they were on break from filming different movies. Enrico played his saxophone accompanied by a girl on harmonica. Nearby, some of the girls jumped rope while a group of boys played tag. When Hadley walked toward them, they stopped what they were doing and looked at her in awe.

Nick stepped forward to speak for the group. "All of us tried to resist Maxine and Charmaine, and all of us failed." He smiled ruefully. "But enough is enough. They have to be stopped," he said. "And you're just the one to do it, Hadley. We know you can." The rest of the kids smiled and pulled her in for a group hug. She felt their arms around her and the warmth of their love. The feeling stayed with her even after she woke up.

She spent the next day still imprisoned in her room. First thing in the morning, Aunt Charmaine brought her a glass of water, and by the afternoon the roaches had managed to snag some crackers for her, but it wasn't enough. She thought of her refrigerator at home filled to the brim with delicious food and beverages. Next to the fridge on the counter was always a cluster of bananas and (very often) alongside it a plate of freshly baked blueberry muffins. Her mouth watered at the thought. With any luck, she'd be home before the day was over.

When she heard Aunt Charmaine's key in the lock, she was ready. "Showtime," Hadley whispered to the roaches, flexing her fingers. They were out of sight by the time the door opened.

"How are you doing, Hadley?" Aunt Charmaine asked.

"Never better." She slid off the bed, glad she had her dancing shoes on, and was ready to go. Aunt Charmaine trudged down the stairs as if her joints pained her. Hadley danced down behind her, each stair one step closer to her victory dance.

Aunt Charmaine stopped and turned back, saying, "Aren't you the energetic one." She raised one eyebrow, a suspicious look crossing her face.

Hadley said, "Yes, Aunt Charmaine."

"Remember, no more shenanigans or Maxine will have your hide. Understand?"

"I understand, Aunt Charmaine. No more shenanigans." The word "shenanigans" made Hadley smile. It sounded like a word that would describe a monkey or toddler. There were better words for what Hadley had in mind: Victory. Conquest. Domination. The aunts would soon find that it had been a mistake to underestimate her.

When they got to the parlor, Aunt Maxine stood waiting. Her face was even more stern than usual, her gray curls, tight as springs, hanging on either side of her face. Hadley nodded as she walked past, ready to take her place in the center of the room, but Aunt Maxine had other plans.

"Not so fast," she said, grabbing hold of Hadley's ear. "We need to talk."

"Yes, Aunt Maxine," Hadley said, her breath catching in her chest. From the corner of her eye, she thought she caught sight of a pair of green glowing eyes peeking out from behind the curtains, but it was just for an instant and then it was gone. Still gripping her ear, Aunt Maxine marched Hadley across the room. When she let go, Hadley straightened up and waited.

"This is your last chance," Aunt Maxine said. "And if you try to pull anything, it will be over for you. I've been more than forgiving, and I'm out of patience." She sat down in her chair, and now they were at eye level.

"Yes, Aunt Maxine."

"What is it you understand?"

"All of it."

"Tell me exactly."

Hadley tipped her head to one side, trying to remember. "You said that this is my last chance. If I try to pull anything, it will be over for me. You've been more than forgiving, and you're out of patience."

"Hmm." Aunt Maxine crossed her arms. Despite the fact that Hadley had perfectly repeated the words, she didn't look pleased.

Aunt Charmaine, over by the Victrola, called out, "Maxine, I think she understands. Can't we just let her dance?" She put the platter on the turntable and cranked the handle. Hadley took her cue and went to the center of the room. She fought the urge to look up at the chandelier. There would be time for that later.

The music began, and Aunt Charmaine trundled over to take her seat. Hadley raised her arms over her head. Right at that moment, nerves set in and she felt her stomach constrict in panic, but she took a deep breath and talked herself through it. She reminded herself that it was okay that Gigi and company were nowhere in sight. That's how it was supposed to be. She was going to be fine, just fine. She envisioned her mother looking her in the eyes and saying what she did before every performance: *No one expects you to be perfect. Just do your best and make it matter.*

Hadley took a deep breath and let the music flow through her body. Ba da da da dum, tra la, tra la! She closed her eyes and began, her feet and arms moving in time with the music. So much depended on things that were out of her control, but she wouldn't think about any of that just now.

She and the music were one. Around the room she felt a wave of love that mirrored what she'd felt in the dream. Enrico, Mary, John Paul, Amaya, Milton, Tracy, Derek, Abner, Cora, Pearl, Herbert, Bertha, Ethel, and Nicholas. It was as if the other children were with her in spirit, surrounding her with love and support. Even if it was just her imagination, thinking it was so made her feel better. She heard the rustling of a million roaches just outside the room, in the walls, behind the curtains, under the furniture, waiting for her cue.

"Why is the idiot girl smiling?" Aunt Maxine said in a loud aside to her sister.

Aunt Charmaine waved away the question. "Who knows? Who cares? There's no law against being happy."

And Hadley danced, perfectly in sync with the music, swaying from side to side as if her life depended on it. Above her the light felt her energy and came to life, flickering and buzzing, a chandelier dragon ready to devour her. But not today. Today she would be the one slaying the dragon.

Hadley paused to snap her fingers like a flamenco dancer, and nodded her head to the roaches. Gigi and the rest of them were all around her, but still in hiding. She began to count aloud, "One, two, three..."

"Why is she counting?" Aunt Maxine leaned over to ask her sister. "It's distracting."

But Hadley wasn't stopping. "Four, five, six, seven, eight..."

The rustling got louder as roaches came from every corner of the house, converging in the parlor all at once. They flew, they scurried, they ran and leaped. Within seconds, millions of green glowing eyes filled the room with glittering luminescence. One moment, there was no sign of roaches; the next, they were everywhere. The floor, the walls, the ceiling. Even the horn and base of the Victrola were decorated with dots of glimmering green eyes. Hadley clasped her hands together. Their timing was magnificent.

The aunts screamed and jumped up onto their chairs, but there was no getting away from the bugs. "Make it stop, sister," Aunt Charmaine yelled.

Maxine swatted at the bugs and tried to step on them, but they were too quick and ran out from underneath her feet before she could crush them. "Get out!" she screamed, her face red as a tomato.

Hadley pumped a fist in the air. On cue, the roaches gathered together and, working to become one, created a pyramid base which pushed Hadley up to the top. She was the captain of the roach cheerleading squad. As they took their positions, surrounding and cradling her, the roaches lifted Hadley up into the air. She rose higher and higher, as cradled and safe as a baby in a mother's arms. Glancing down, she watched the room get smaller, the aunts' attention solely on the bugs, who had now infiltrated their clothing and hair. They frantically swatted and wriggled but couldn't get away from them.

Aunt Maxine tried to run out of the room, but the roaches had linked their legs together to create a wall blocking the doorway. She bounced off the roach wall and waved her arms around her head as she frantically ran in circles.

Aunt Charmaine hit at herself and shook her head, trying to get the roaches out of her ears and nose. They perched on her head and swung from curl to curl, chittering as they went. "There's so many of them," she cried. "Why are there so many of them?"

Gigi, who was perched on Hadley's shoulder, spoke into her ear. "What a stupid question. There are so many of us because we propagate quickly!"

When Hadley reached the chandelier, she grabbed hold of the chain and yanked on it. She was close enough now to see the jagged crack in the ceiling from her efforts the day before. Plaster dust filtered down as she pulled, but as much as she tried, she wasn't strong enough to tear it out of the ceiling.

The dust drifted down, catching Aunt Charmaine's attention. "Sister, stop her!" she cried, one gnarled finger pointing upward.

CHAPTER 17

Hadley tugged at the chain with all her might. *Come on, come on, come on,* she silently begged, but the light fixture didn't budge. Down below she spotted Aunt Maxine charging toward the center of the room. "Look out!" Hadley yelled, calling out an alarm to her roach friends.

Aunt Maxine rammed her body against the roach pyramid, scattering them across the room. At that same moment, Hadley swung her legs over the bottom frame of the chandelier and pulled herself up to a seating position. She gripped each side of the fixture like she was sitting on a swing. The prisms clinked together like wind chimes.

"Get her down!" Aunt Charmaine screamed.

Aunt Maxine bellowed, and the sound filled the room, echoing off the walls. Her outstretched arm reached for Hadley. "I will end you," she screamed, her open mouth black as a cave. She reached for Hadley, but her fingers just brushed the soles of her feet.

Hadley scooted away from Aunt Maxine's outstretched hands and swung the chandelier around. She kicked her feet, infuriating the old woman even more. The roaches still covered both of the aunts, causing them to shake their heads and flick their hands over themselves, but their eyes were on the chandelier. Hadley tried to climb higher, hoping to reach the part where the fixture was attached to the ceiling, but she couldn't manage a foothold.

"Sister, drag the table over," Charmaine said in excitement. "We'll beat her at her own game."

The two got on either side of the table and moved it directly below Hadley. Aunt Charmaine tried to clamber on top but couldn't get her knee up high enough. She pulled up her skirt and tried again, this time trying the other leg. "Can you give me a lift, Maxine?" she asked in frustration.

Aunt Maxine came around to her side of the table, but instead of helping her sister, she shoved her hip against her, knocking her down.

Sprawled on the floor among the roaches, Aunt Charmaine was a circle of light blue fabric in a sea of green glittering eyes. "Not nice!" she said, tears in her voice. "Why can't you ever be nice?"

Aunt Maxine didn't answer. Instead, she stared up at Hadley, her eyes two piercing dark holes. "Now you're going to pay, little girl. You're going to be the sorriest child who's ever lived."

Hadley tugged at the chain. "Gigi, a little help here?" she begged. "I need to get this chain pulled loose." She'd lost sight of Gigi, and all of the roaches looked the same to her now.

Gigi flew onto her shoulder. "I'm on it!" She let out a whistle, and a swarm of roaches flew up, encircled the top of the chandelier, and began to nibble at the chain links.

Right below her, Aunt Maxine jumped onto the table like a lion pouncing on its prey. Hadley's heart knocked in her chest. She was running out of time to take down the chandelier. "Faster, faster," she cried, encouraging the roaches who gnawed at the metal links, but the chain looked untouched.

Aunt Maxine leaped up and grabbed for Hadley's foot. "It's over."

Hadley screamed and tried to pull her foot away, but the old lady's grip was tight. There was nowhere to go. Oh why did she think this would work? Even a million roaches weren't able to help her. She gulped back a sob and again attempted to jerk away, but her foot was getting squeezed now, every tiny, precious bone in danger of being crushed. She yelped in pain and clutched at the chandelier, pulling off one of the prisms in the process.

"It's. Over," Aunt Maxine repeated, a smug look on her face.

"No!" said Hadley, clutching the prism in her hand. And then, as hard as she could, she threw the prism down at Aunt Maxine.

She had thought she might catch Aunt Maxine off guard and buy herself a little more time. What she didn't expect was the way the prism shattered into a million brilliant rays of light the second it hit the old woman's shoulder. For a moment the entire room filled with a blinding flash accompanied by the jaunty strains of a harmonica. Aunt Maxine jumped back as if stung. "Stop it right now," she screamed.

Aunt Charmaine grabbed a lamp and lunged forward, aiming straight for Hadley's dangling legs. All around, the roaches twittered, "Watch out, Hadley! She's coming. Watch out!"

They swarmed over Aunt Charmaine, who paid them no mind but charged with the lamp straight ahead of her like a battering ram.

Hadley frantically pulled at the prisms, and as they came loose, she hurled them across the room. With each downed prism, the room filled with light, and a series of sounds filled the air: the bleating of a trumpet, the metallic click of tap shoes, the whoosh of juggling clubs, a boy doing card tricks.

The aunts cried out, "No, Hadley. Stop!" But Hadley wasn't afraid of them anymore. From where she sat, it looked like they were shrinking. Somehow they were becoming smaller and less threatening.

The prisms were so grateful to be free, Hadley couldn't stop. She snatched at more and more, and as they hit the table and the floor, they filled the room with bursts of light and the sounds of singing and a saxophone and other joyful noises. She couldn't leave even one prism untouched. When she'd thrown every last one, she stopped to look down. The roaches had scurried off to each side of the room. Aunt Charmaine sat on the floor, while Aunt Maxine slumped against the wall.

"You wicked, wicked girl," Aunt Charmaine said, her neck craning upward. "You couldn't just go along, could you?"

"You took what wasn't yours," Hadley said, looking down from her perch. "You had to be stopped."

Aunt Maxine shook her head. "All we wanted was to live forever. Was that so wrong?"

"And all I wanted was to go home," Hadley said. "I didn't think *that* was asking for much."

Aunt Maxine said, "It's always about you. Isn't it, Hadley?"

"Selfish girl," Aunt Charmaine said.

"Stupid, selfish girl," Aunt Maxine said. "Doesn't know her place."

Both the aunts were drooping now, resembling crayons left out in the sun. Their gray curls sagged, and their clothing hung shapelessly on their bodies, as if they'd recently lost a lot of weight. The skin on their faces bulged in odd places, and the bones in their hands jutted out at the ends of their fingertips. Aunt Maxine spoke in a slur as if falling asleep. "All we wanted was to live forever."

Gigi tapped at Hadley's forehead to get her attention and flew a few inches from her face, pointing upward. "Hey Hadley, we did it!" Hadley looked up to see the roaches still working on the chandelier's chain. She'd never told them to stop, so they'd just kept going. One section of the links had been chewed away so it was now only the width of a thread. Three of the roaches were still nibbling at it while several others hovered nearby, admiring their work. "Good job! Keep going! Don't give up!"

"Wait!" Hadley said. "I don't need–" But before she got the words out, the roaches broke through the rest of the metal. She and the chandelier fell, first with one short jolt as the link expanded and then a sudden sharp drop until she plummeted to the floor, landing with a thunderous crack.

CHAPTER 18

The sensation of falling. A whirl of kaleidoscope colors. The whoosh of a wind tunnel. And then complete darkness. Far, far in the distance she heard one last tiny wail from Aunt Maxine, "All I wanted was to live forever..."

In the darkness, Hadley became a girl adrift on a cushion of air. She felt herself being pulled headfirst away from Grimm House. All around her only darkness. But it was a good darkness, one that felt safe and full of possibility. It was the darkness of a heavy blanket on a cold night. The darkness of a mother's hand on her forehead when she had a fever. The darkness of a summer night's sky. She relaxed, and even though she didn't know what was happening, she trusted that all would be well. When she felt herself land, it felt good just to sit and let her weary body rest.

The quiet welcomed her. The darkness became the back of her closed eyelids. She wasn't sure how much time had elapsed when she heard a voice. "Hadley? Are you okay?" Someone gently touched her shoulder. She opened her eyes to see Zoe looming above her.

Hadley looked around and got her bearings. They were in the basement of Graham Place, in her family's storage room. She was sitting on the concrete floor, her back against the chicken-wire wall, her legs outstretched in front of her. Dance shoes adorned her feet. A slant of afternoon light coming in through the windows on the opposite side of the basement made her blink.

"Are you okay?" Zoe asked again.

"Yes, I'm..." Hadley struggled to her feet. She saw her iPod and speakers on the floor nearby. Had she been practicing? No, she decided. She'd been away and just now returned. Plucked out of the nightmare that was Grimm House and dropped back into her own life. "I guess I just fell asleep."

"You looked dead," Zoe said. "I was ready to call 911." She had her cell phone in her hand.

"No, I'm alive," Hadley said, and the words opened up a wellspring of joy. She was alive and back in her own world. She threw back her head and laughed. "I'm alive and I'm home."

"Good for you," Zoe said, sounding bored. She held up the phone. "Your parents called from the airport. They'll be home soon."

Hadley snatched the phone out of her hand and put it up to her ear. "Mom, Mom, is that you?"

"They're not on the phone *now*." Zoe grabbed the phone and wiped it against the front of her shirt. "They called earlier, but you were down here, so I took a message."

Her mother had told Zoe that they'd decided to cut the trip short because Hadley's father had been seasick the entire time. Zoe went on to relate the conversation in between snaps of her gum. "Your mom said the whole thing was a complete misery. At the first port, they left the ship and booked a flight home. They're at the airport now. They'll be home soon, so you better hurry and get your room straightened out."

As Hadley bounded up the stairs, she said, "I can't wait to see them."

"Me too," Zoe said, trailing behind her. "Once they pay me, I'll get my life back."

An hour later, when her parents walked through the door, dropping their suitcases, Hadley couldn't hold back. She rushed to greet them, crying out, "I'm so happy you're home." Her mother gave her a long hug, and her father picked her up and swung her around the way he used to when she was little. Once Zoe was paid and out the door, it was just the three of them. The world as it should be.

At the dinner table that evening, her mother caught Hadley grinning at them and said, "I guess we should go away more often. Our daughter has a new appreciation for us."

"It's not a *new* appreciation," Hadley said. "I always appreciated you."

She appreciated the apartment too. She walked from room to room, sinking her toes into the soft rugs and breathing in the clean air. The windows were spotless. In the kitchen, she admired all the choices in the refrigerator. Juice and grapes and leftover chicken! Apples and a strawberry-rhubarb torte. A plastic container filled with chopped salad. Cheese and yogurt and lemonade. All of the foods she'd thought about during her stay at Grimm House were now in front of her, and she could eat any and all of it if she wanted to. So very extravagant. Her mother peeked around the door, "Are you still hungry or are you just letting all the cold air out?"

Hadley closed the door. "Just checking my options."

As the evening wore on, the memory of Grimm House began to feel distant, like a movie she'd once seen. The details were getting fuzzy. Would she soon forget her time there, like all the other children? She practiced a few dance moves in her studio, relieved to find out nothing had changed. If anything, her love of dancing was stronger than ever before. As it turned out, almost losing her passion had made her treasure it all the more.

That night, she asked her parents to tuck her in the way they did in her younger years. Her mother adjusted the covers while her father pretended to check under the bed and in the closet for monsters, something she was more thankful for than she'd wanted to admit. "Love you, Mom and Dad," she said as they gave her one last hug and kiss.

Her mother stepped back and gave her a long look. "Is there something you want to tell us?"

Hadley said, "Like what?"

"I don't know." Her mother tapped her chin. "Something's off. You seem different. You know you can tell us anything, no matter what."

For a split second, Hadley considered spilling the whole story, but something held her back. How could she explain what had happened without sounding crazy? She wasn't even sure she understood it herself. And saying the words out loud would make it real, giving it power. "No, everything's fine. I'm just glad you're back."

"Believe me, we're glad too." Her father came back for one last kiss on her forehead, and then the lights were turned off and the door closed.

As Hadley drifted off to sleep, she heard faint noises off in the distance. The bleat of a trumpet, the click of tap shoes, voices raised in song, and the wail of a saxophone. A thank you note of sounds. The joyful succession continued: a deck being shuffled, a magician calling out, "Is this your card?" and a harmonica playing a happy tune. And then a hushed voice reciting a poem. She couldn't quite make out the words. Still, it made her smile.

CHAPTER 19

At breakfast the next morning, after Hadley mentioned having left her music in their storage space, her father reached over and gave her arm a squeeze. "If you're scared to go down, you know one of us would go with you." The lines next to his eyes crinkled as he gave her a supportive smile. "Just say the word."

Hadley took a deep breath. Was she afraid? She'd never liked the basement, and now she associated it with her nightmarish visit to the aunts. But here at the breakfast table, her father sipping his coffee, her mother bustling around in the kitchen, she felt protected. Things had shifted inside of her too. She'd defeated the dragon chandelier and by her wits alone had found her way home. Any girl who could do that was nearly invincible. Surely she could retrieve some items from the basement. "I'm not afraid," she said. "I'll go down after I'm done eating."

This is not a big deal, Hadley told herself as she stepped into the elevator thirty minutes later. When Mrs. Knapp and her little terrier Chester got on at the second floor, Hadley found herself reaching down to scratch the dog behind the ears. "That's a good puppy," she said even though Chester had not been a puppy for a very long time. "Such a good boy."

"It's a lovely day," Mrs. Knapp said, looking over her glasses. "Going outdoors?"

"No," Hadley said. "I'm going to get something out of the basement."

Mrs. Knapp said, "The basement? By yourself? Aren't you the brave one! It's creepy down there." They both got off on the first floor. "Have a good day," Mrs. Knapp said cheerily as Chester led the way to the street entrance. Hadley passed Clyde the doorman, who gave her a nod. He and the white-haired elderly man who stood next to him were intently watching a sports event on a tiny screen propped up on the counter. Sometimes the doormen asked what she wanted and offered to help, but not this time. She was on her own.

Not a big deal, she thought, bounding down the stairs. Tenants in the building went into the basement all the time. Nothing bad had ever happened to them as far as she knew. It was just a damp basement in an old building. Nothing more, nothing less.

When Hadley turned the corner at the bottom of the stairs, she did a double take, wondering just for a second if she was in the right place. The basement was no longer dimly lit. Instead circular work lamps were clamped to the support beams on the ceiling, making the space as bright as day. A pile of possessions blocked the aisle to her family's storage room. From the stack of boxes, tarp-covered furniture, and other loose odds and ends, it looked like someone was moving. Under the bright lights, this area looked less like something from a horror movie and more like a standard basement. She had let her fears get away from her. The basement was just a basement: cement walls, a furnace, the old incinerator, and water boiler.

She stepped around the piles, so intent on getting her iPod that she didn't even see the boy until he was right in front of her. "Hello," he said. He had shaggy brown hair and oversized jeans cuffed at the bottom. His T-shirt was white with a streak of dirt on the front. There was a green backpack at his feet.

"Sorry," she said. "I didn't see you there."

"I know you," he said. "You're the dancer."

"And I know you," she said. "You're the boy who was spying on me through the window."

"I wasn't spying," he hastily exclaimed. "I mean, I know it looked like spying, but that wasn't what I was trying to do."

Hadley folded her arms in front of her. "So what were you trying to do?"

"My grandfather bought this building, and we were inspecting the windows. I didn't mean to keep looking, but your dancing was so great! I've never seen anyone dance that good. I just couldn't stop watching."

She looked at his expressive, earnest face and said, "Thank you." She felt embarrassed and flattered at the same time. It was a good feeling all the same.

"Did you come down to see the stuff we found?" He gestured to the pile behind him. Technically, he was part of the pile since he was sitting on one of the boxes.

Hadley looked where he'd pointed. "What? No. I left my iPod in my family's storage room yesterday. I hope it's still there." She glanced down the row in that direction even though it was impossible to see something on the floor from where she stood.

"An iPod and speakers?" The boy asked. "In an empty storage room with the door wide open so anyone could have taken it?"

"Yes," Hadley said, eagerly. "That's it. Did you see it?"

He nodded. "It had a name on the case? Hadley something? My grandfather took it upstairs and gave it to the doorman for safekeeping."

"I'm Hadley."

"I thought so." He grinned, revealing his braces. "My grandfather just bought this apartment building. My family is going to move into number 201."

Zoe's apartment, Hadley realized with a smile. So she really *was* moving. No wonder she'd been so grouchy.

The boy said, "Today I'm helping Grandpa work in the basement." The water boiler kicked in, making a familiar rushing, clanking sound. Hadley turned her head and listened. The boy continued his explanation. "The building custodian started up the incinerator for us so we can burn things."

"Is this your grandfather's stuff?" Hadley asked, toeing a box. The pile reached up to the ceiling.

"No, it's from a storage space no one is claiming. My grandpa thinks this stuff has been here forever. He lived here when he was a kid, and he remembers seeing it then."

Hadley said, "I only came down for my things, and since they're upstairs now..." She turned to leave.

"Oh, don't go!" The boy jumped up. "Want to see something really cool?"

Hadley gave it a thought, flipping back and forth between wanting to leave and wondering about the really cool thing. When it came down to it, if she'd left at that point, she'd never know what she missed. "Sure."

He beckoned with one finger. "Over here." She followed him back around the pile, stopping when they reached a mound set off to one side and covered by a gray tarp. It was about the size of a small coffee table. "Check this out." He whipped the cloth off to reveal a miniature building.

Not any miniature building though. It was a scaled-down replica of Graham Place. Not an exact recreation, though. This version had a front door with a rounded top and decorative metal bars on each of the windows. A dark green car with a crank on the front was parked by the front door. Hadley went to pick up the model car, but it was stuck. "I tried that too," the boy said. "The crank turns, but the car is attached somehow."

Hadley nodded and walked around the small building, speechless. In the back, where there was now parking and a small garden in the real Graham Place, the replica had a fenced area with trees so large they almost completely obscured the ground.

The boy excitedly filled her in. "It's the apartment building back in the day when it was a mansion and this rich family lived here. This is what it looked like before they divided it up into apartments."

"I didn't know that one family lived here to begin with." Hadley felt a click in her brain. Something was starting to make sense.

"Pretty cool, huh?" he said. "I found this the other day, but we didn't figure out how to open it up and see all the rooms until this morning."

"It opens up?" She tried to look into one of the windows, but it was impossible to see inside. She put one fingertip through the window bars and tapped against the glass.

"Wait till you see." He crouched down next to her and released a latch under the edge of the roof, then did the same on the other side. He flipped the roof back, revealing the inside of the house from above, then went to work doing the same thing to the front of the model, which swung open like a door.

Hadley saw that the miniature was exactly like Grimm House. Each room overflowed with dark, ancient furniture. The grandfather clock with no hands stood in the front hall, just as she remembered it. Each window had heavy tapestry curtains pulled back with gold cords, except they were teeny tiny now. The hallways twisted and turned, lined with paintings of old men with creepy eyes. She remembered walking down those halls, afraid of the eyes that appeared to be following her. Strange to see it so small. It looked harmless when brought down to size.

As her eyes flitted over the interior, a bit of movement and the sight of two green glowing eyes distracted her. It was Gigi, winking at Hadley from the corner of one room. She was her usual size, which made her look enormous in the miniature house. Hadley grinned at her and mouthed "thank you." Gigi rose up on her hind legs and gave Hadley a wave of her antennae in return. And then, right before Hadley's eyes, she raced out of the house and sprinted across the basement floor. Hadley turned her head to look and saw as Gigi joined a group of other roaches, all of whom disappeared into one of the storage spaces.

Luckily, the boy didn't notice. "You can see that this is where the elevator is now," he said, pointing. "And they did lots of other stuff too when they switched it to an apartment building. They added some walls and took some away. Added some doors. You would hardly know it was the same place."

"So who owned the house, back when it was a mansion?" she asked.

"These super rich people. The Grahams."

"What happened to them?"

He shrugged. "Died off? Not really sure. The last ones to own the place were these two old ladies. Sisters. They never got married, I guess."

Hadley knelt down on the concrete floor to look into the rooms on the first floor. Her eyes followed the carpet runner from the dining room to the parlor. It was just as she'd left it. She felt another click of understanding. A Victrola stood between two stuffed wing chairs. The library table was still in the middle of the room underneath a thin wisp of wire sticking out of the ceiling. Bits of what looked like glitter covered the room. What was left of the prism energy. Hadley herself was missing of course, along with the part of the chandelier she'd been sitting on when she crashed down from the ceiling.

She looked in the corners and saw two people-shaped figures wrapped in faded blue cloth, gray yarn protruding out of the lumps at the top. Tiny replicas of Aunt Maxine and Aunt Charmaine. She drew back but then remembered: *they can't hurt me anymore.* Boldly she reached in and picked one up. The part that would have been a face resembled a potato more than a human being. It was impossible to tell if it had been Maxine or Charmaine. "What's this?" she asked, holding it in her outstretched palm.

"My grandpa thinks it's supposed to be the sisters who lived here," he said. "They used to make dolls out of wax way back when. It looks like they got all messed up from being stored down here."

Hadley put the ruined doll back next to the other one. They'd been close in real life and wanted to live forever. She didn't think living as a deformed doll was what they had in mind, but it was what they deserved. She picked up the Victrola and gave it a close look before putting it back again. Something slimy covered the surface. When she pressed on the carpet runner in the hallway, it felt damp.

Hadley felt the final click. Shrunk down to dollhouse size, Grimm House looked innocent, but she knew better. When she was there, it was anything but harmless. She couldn't decide what had happened—was it once large and then became smaller, or had she been the one to get shrunken? Was it possible that she'd never actually left the building? Trying to figure all this out made her brain hurt. Either way, Aunt Maxine had knocked on her door, her actual real-world door, and taken her away. If given the chance, they would have stolen her greatest treasure. Her love and talent for dance would have been gone forever.

Worse yet, they threatened to end her, to banish her to nothingness. There couldn't be anything worse than that.

She'd managed to free herself and take down the chandelier, but what if she hadn't entirely destroyed the evil? Maybe in some way it still existed, right here in front of her. She imagined another child being sucked into the world of Grimm House, dealing with the aunts whose now-misshapen faces were devoid of eyes and nose and mouth. A chilling thought.

CHAPTER 20

The sound of heavy footsteps on the basement stairs interrupted her thoughts. A man's voice rang out. "Connor! Connor, my boy! Are you there?"

The boy stood up, wiped the front of his jeans and called out, "Yes, Grandpa!"

Hadley got to her feet too, recognizing the grandfather's voice and the boy's name. A memory stirred in her brain, and she could see herself talking through the fence at the aunts' house to someone who didn't talk back. And when that anonymous someone was called away, she had learned his name, his full name. What were the chances it would be the same person? She tugged on the boy's T-shirt. "Are you Connor McAvoy?"

He smiled, a glint coming off his braces. "Yep, that's me."

Before she could say any more, Connor's grandfather came around the corner. Hadley recognized him as the man who'd been watching the game with Clyde, the doorman. He looked like a grandfather, Hadley decided, the sort of kindly grandfather you'd see in a movie. His hair and mustache were white and full, his cheeks were pink, and he had wire-rim glasses. He wore jeans and a tan workman's shirt. Connor's grandfather stopped short when he noticed Hadley. "Oh, you found a friend," he said, sounding delighted.

"This is Hadley," Connor said. "She lives in the building. She's the one I told you about. The girl who dances."

"Ah." The old man nodded his head. "The girl who dances. Connor has been talking about you a lot." Now it was Connor's turn to look sheepish. His grandpa said, "Would you also be Hadley of the iPod and speakers?"

"Yes." Hadley said.

"Clyde has them up at the front desk," he said.

Hadley said, "I'm usually very careful with my things. I just forgot yesterday."

Connor's grandfather smiled. "I understand. I forget things all the time." He motioned to the basement. "Sometimes you need reminders. I lived in Graham Place when I was a kid and being back here now is bringing up all kinds of memories." He put his hands on his hips and sighed. "But enough small talk. Time to get to work."

"Are we cleaning the doll house?" Connor asked.

His grandfather shook his head. "No, it can't be salvaged." He explained that everything damp and mildewed was a health risk. The big pieces of furniture would be picked up by a company that specialized in hazardous waste. The smaller items could be discarded, or burned, as long as they were careful. He leaned down and unzipped the green backpack, then pulled out facemasks and gloves. "If you're sticking around, Hadley, you'll need to wear these," he said, handing her a mask and a pair of gloves.

She watched as Connor and his grandfather pulled on their masks and gloves and put hers on the same way. Connor's grandpa opened the incinerator door, and together the two guys carefully lifted the model of Grimm House. Hadley could tell it was heavy by how they handled it.

"Are you sure we have to burn it?" Connor said. "It seems like such a cool, old thing."

His grandfather said, "Sometimes things are not what they seem."

Grimm House was perched in the opening to the incinerator. Behind it, Hadley saw the flames waiting to eat it. She felt the heat from five feet away. Connor's grandfather frowned as they positioned the house in the doorway. "It should fit," he said. "It seems to be stuck."

He and Connor wiggled it back and forth, pushing as they went. "It doesn't want to get burned up," Connor observed. "Maybe we should just put it out by the curb?"

"No!" Hadley said. And without even thinking about it, she jumped forward and pushed with both hands. The house gave one last tug of resistance before giving up and sliding into the flames. The fire crackled and sizzled, a fierce, angry noise, then built into a howl of fury. Connor's grandfather slammed the metal door shut and latched it. Inside the incinerator the fire roared as it consumed Grimm House.

Hadley sighed with relief. From start to finish, the deed was done.

As if reading her thoughts, the grandfather said, "It's good to have that over with." He pulled off his mask, looked off in the distance and recited:

Graham Place
Is free once more
Every room and every floor
Top to bottom, door to door
Strange old sisters nevermore

Connor did a double take. "Where did that come from, Grandpa?"

"Huh." The old man looked surprised and pleased. "It just popped into my head out of nowhere. When I was a boy I used to write poems all the time. I gave it up when I was about your age. My mother became very ill and spent a week in the hospital. Even after she came home, it took a long time for her to get her strength back. Somewhere along the way, I lost my knack for writing poetry. Maybe now that I'm retired I'll get back to it."

"Okay," Connor said, but he didn't seem too impressed.

His grandfather grinned. "I had a notebook where I jotted down all my poems. I was going to be a writer when I grew up."

"Maybe you can still be a writer," Hadley said. Behind them the noise of the incinerator settled down—a sign that the miniature house would soon be nothing but ashes.

"Maybe so."

Hadley thought about her parents waiting for her upstairs. She'd been gone far too long already. They might be worried about her. "I should really go," she said. "It was nice meeting you."

"See you around, Hadley," Connor said.

His grandfather said, "It was a pleasure meeting you, young lady. Happy dancing!"

"Thank you!" Hadley said. And then she danced. Up the stairs, across the lobby, into the elevator, and later in her very own dance studio in her very own apartment. No one ever had to make her dance or tell her to practice. She just loved to dance.

A wise bug once told her, "Without passion, life has no meaning." And another smart person, her own mother, had said: "No one expects you to be perfect. Just do your best and make it matter."

As Hadley danced, she reflected on both bits of wisdom. Good advice all around, in dancing and in life.

Made in the USA
Lexington, KY
27 September 2016